FAR OUT
FAIRY TALES

STONE ARCH BOOKS
a capstone imprint

SNOW WHITE

QUEEN REGENT

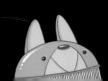

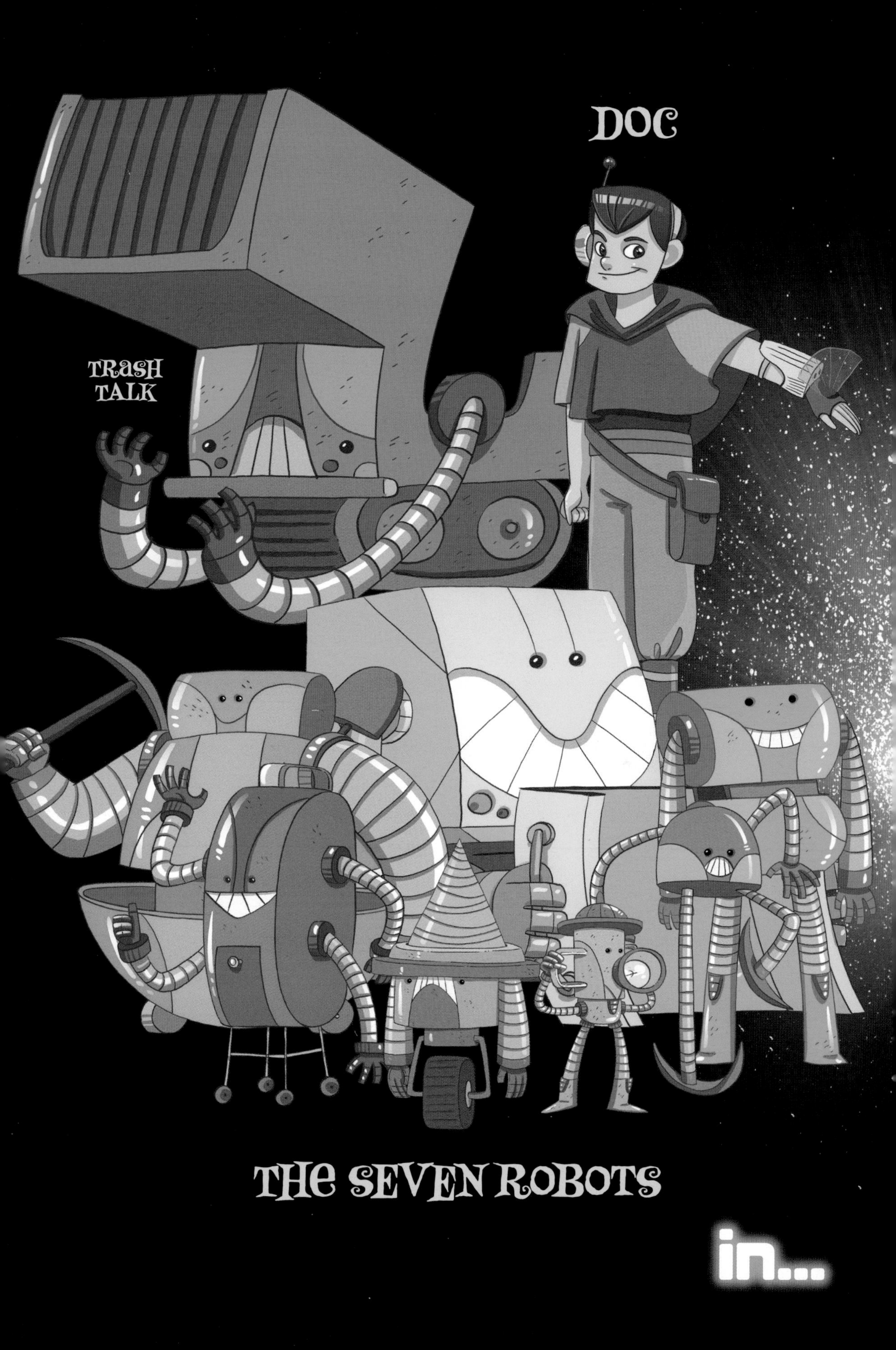
DOC
TRASH TALK
THE SEVEN ROBOTS
in...

Far Out Fairy Tales is published by
Stone Arch Books
A Capstone Imprint
1710 Roe Crest Drive, North Mankato,
Minnesota 56003
www.capstonepub.com

Cataloging-in-Publication Data is
available at the Library of Congress
website.
Hardcover ISBN: 978-1-4342-9648-1
Paperback ISBN: 978-1-4342-9652-8

Summary: On a distant planet called
Techworld, a little girl named Snow
White is created by the planet's
smartest minds to be the perfect
scientist, Snow immediately shows a
knack for working with electronics.
The Queen Regent, fearing for her
crown, exiles Snow White so she
cannot grow up and take the queen's
place as the most intelligent person on
the planet.

Lettering by Jaymes Reed.

Designer: Bob Lentz
Editor: Sean Tulien
Managing Editor: Donald Lemke
Creative Director: Heather Kindseth
Editorial Director: Michael Dahl
Publisher: Ashley C. Andersen Zantop

Printed in the United States of
America in North Mankato, Minnesota.
052018   000482

FAR OUT FAIRY TALES

SNOW WHITE
AND THE
SEVEN ROBOTS

A GRAPHIC NOVEL

BY LOUISE SIMONSON
ILLUSTRATED BY JIMENA SÁNCHEZ

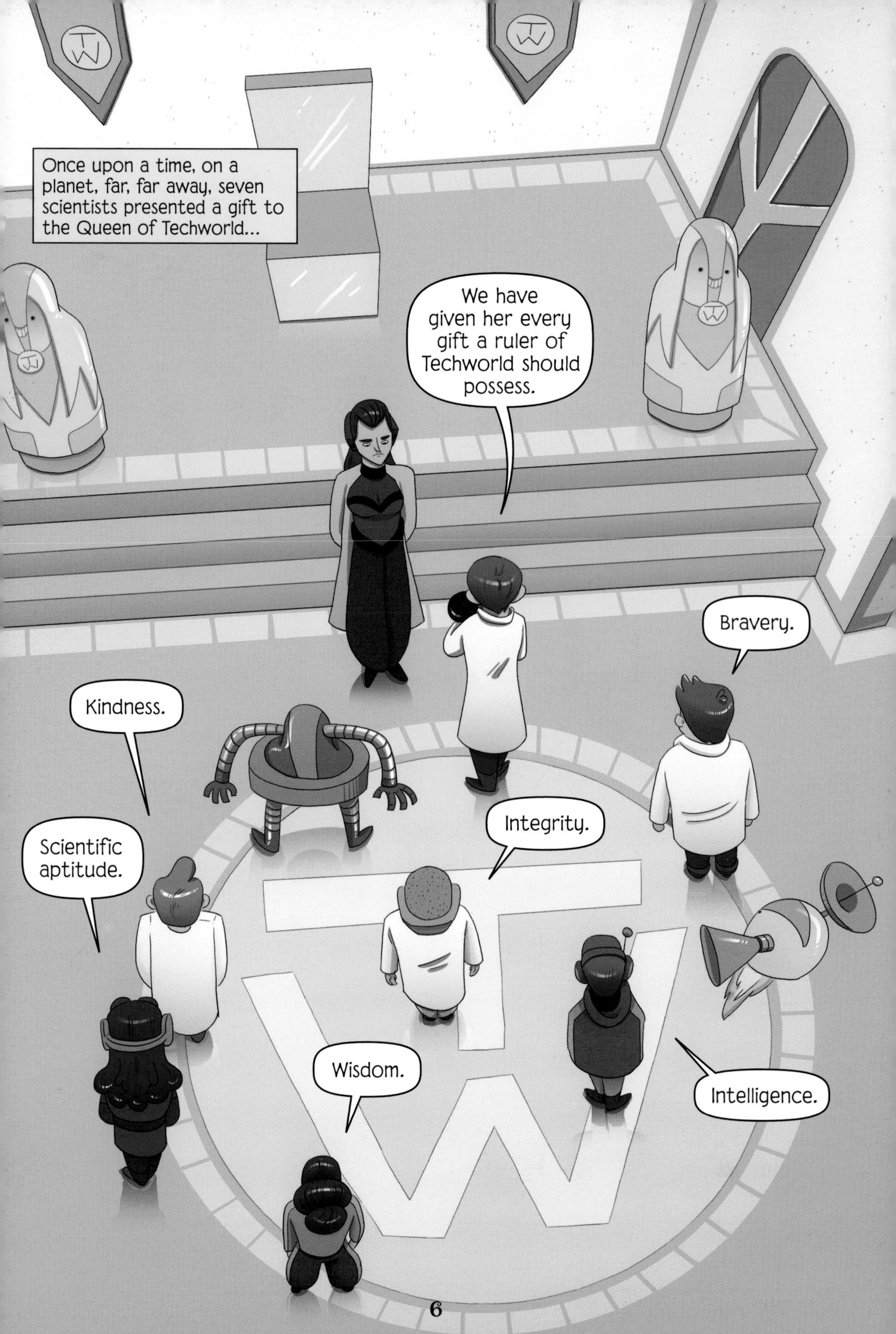

Once upon a time, on a planet, far, far away, seven scientists presented a gift to the Queen of Techworld...
We have given her every gift a ruler of Techworld should possess.
Bravery.
Kindness.
Integrity.
Scientific aptitude.
Wisdom.
Intelligence.

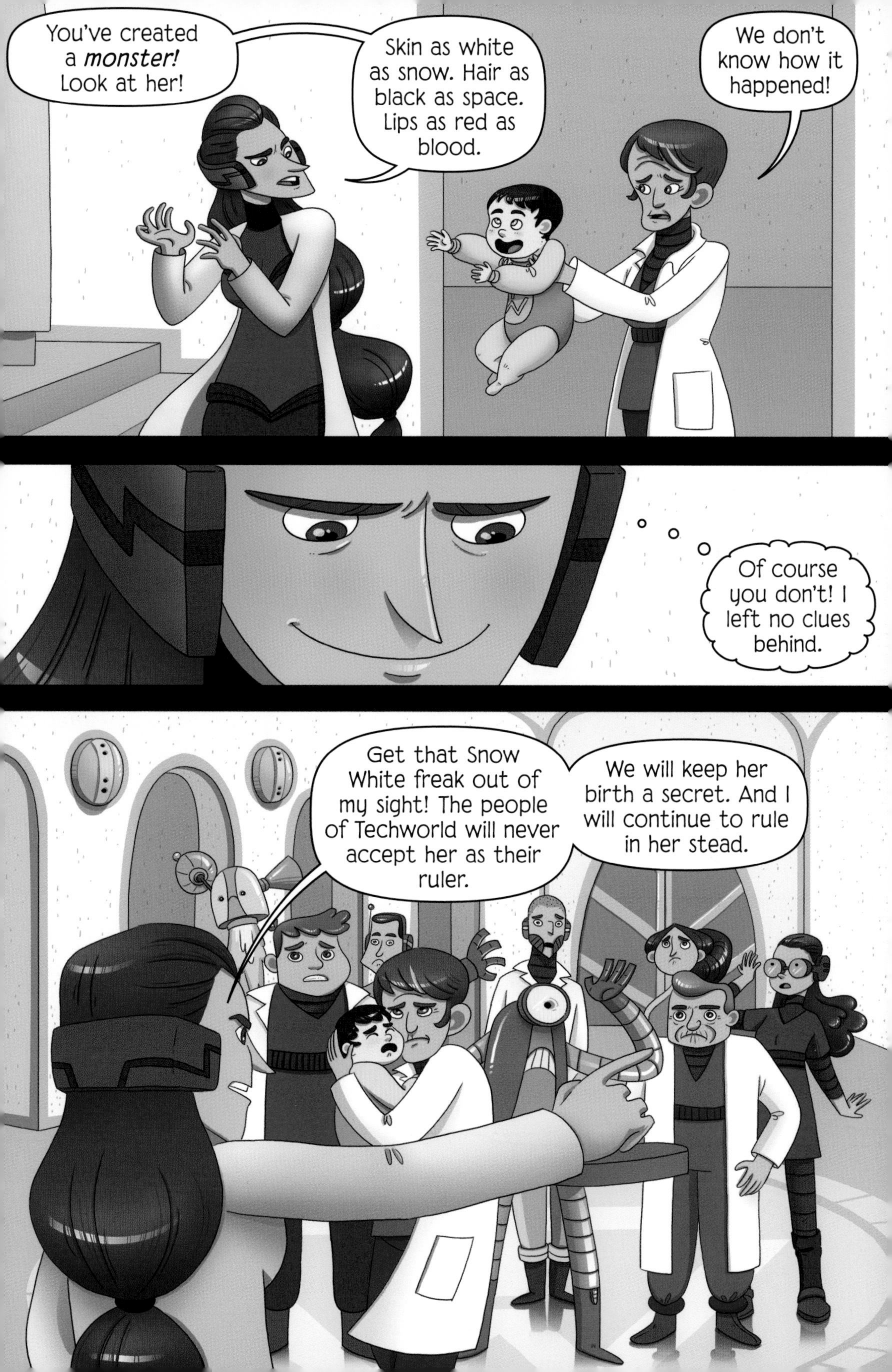
You've created a *monster!* Look at her!
Skin as white as snow. Hair as black as space. Lips as red as blood.
We don't know how it happened!
Of course you don't! I left no clues behind.
Get that Snow White freak out of my sight! The people of Techworld will never accept her as their ruler.
We will keep her birth a secret. And I will continue to rule in her stead.

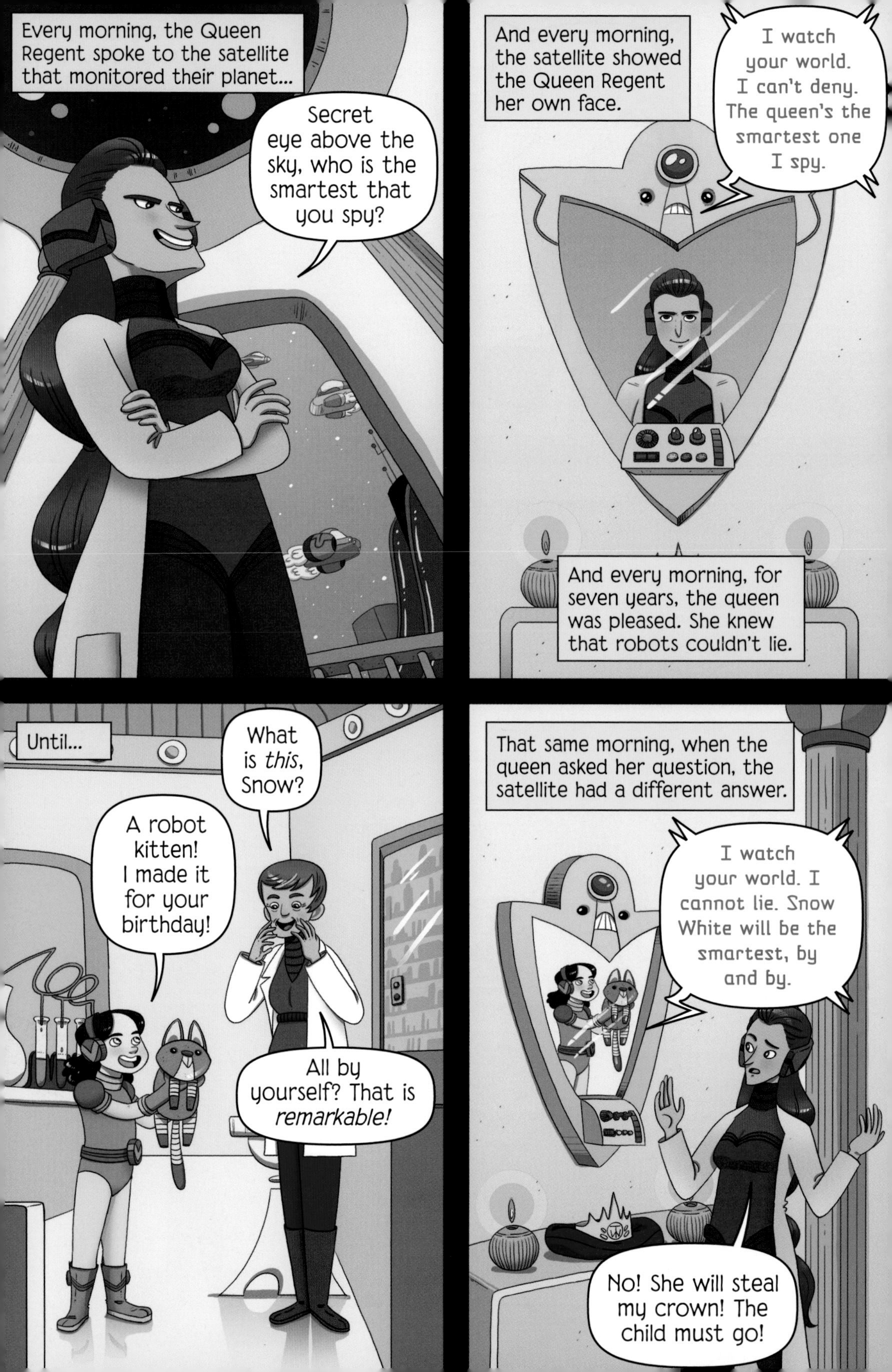

Every morning, the Queen Regent spoke to the satellite that monitored their planet...
Secret eye above the sky, who is the smartest that you spy?
And every morning, the satellite showed the Queen Regent her own face.
I watch your world. I can't deny. The queen's the smartest one I spy.
And every morning, for seven years, the queen was pleased. She knew that robots couldn't lie.
Until...
What is *this*, Snow?
A robot kitten! I made it for your birthday!
All by yourself? That is *remarkable!*
That same morning, when the queen asked her question, the satellite had a different answer.
I watch your world. I cannot lie. Snow White will be the smartest, by and by.
No! She will steal my crown! The child must go!

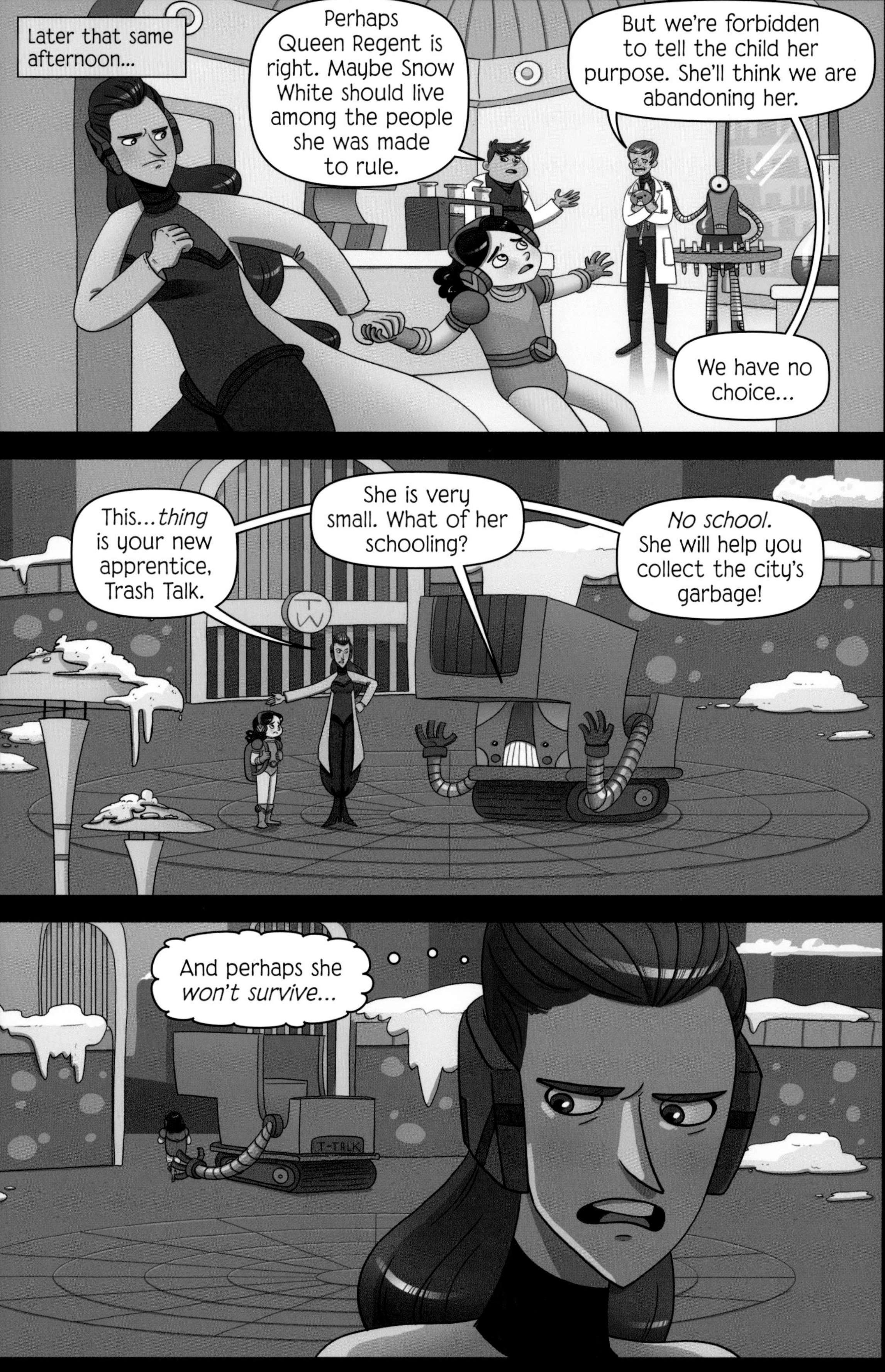
Later that same afternoon...
Perhaps Queen Regent is right. Maybe Snow White should live among the people she was made to rule.
But we're forbidden to tell the child her purpose. She'll think we are abandoning her.
We have no choice...
This...*thing* is your new apprentice, Trash Talk.
She is very small. What of her schooling?
No school. She will help you collect the city's garbage!
T W
And perhaps she *won't survive...*
T-TALK

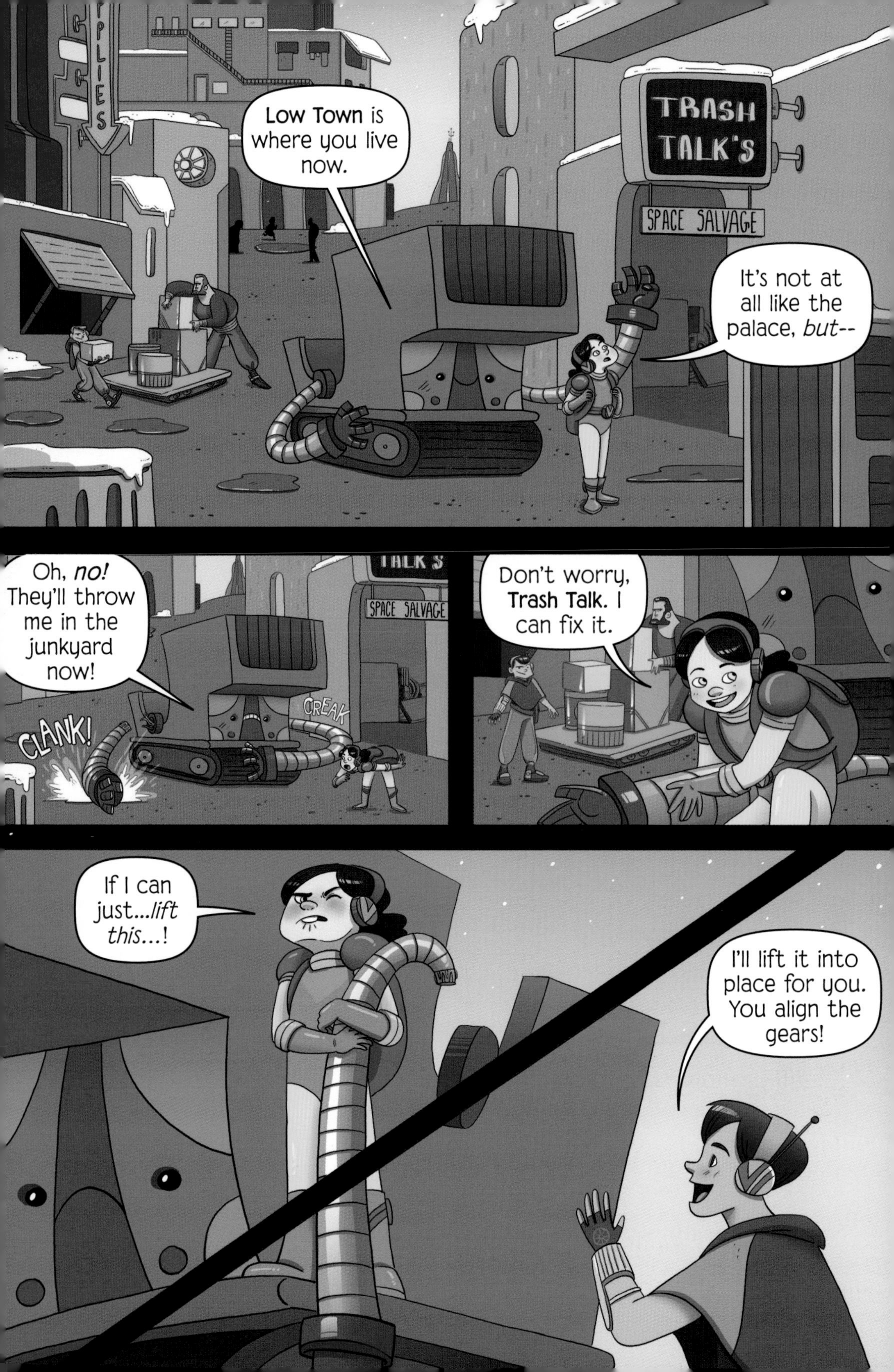
PPLIES
TRASH TALK'S
SPACE SALVAGE
Low Town is where you live now.
It's not at all like the palace, *but*--
TALK'S
SPACE SALVAGE
Oh, *no!* They'll throw me in the junkyard now!
CLANK!
CREAK
Don't worry, Trash Talk. I can fix it.
If I can just...*lift this*...!
I'll lift it into place for you. You align the gears!

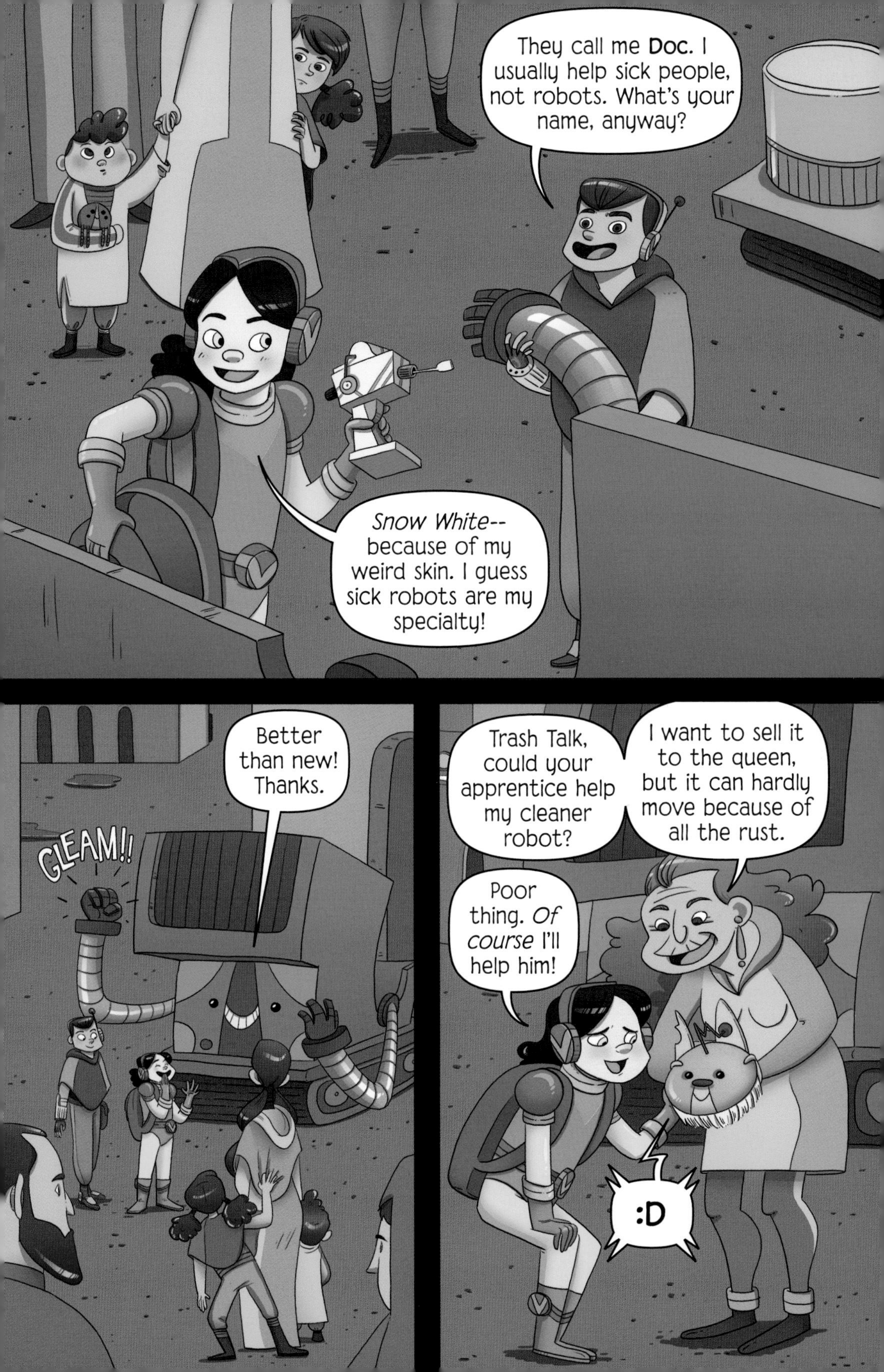
They call me **Doc**. I usually help sick people, not robots. What's your name, anyway?
Snow White-- because of my weird skin. I guess sick robots are my specialty!
Better than new! Thanks.
GLEAM!!
Trash Talk, could your apprentice help my cleaner robot?
I want to sell it to the queen, but it can hardly move because of all the rust.
Poor thing. *Of course* I'll help him!
:D

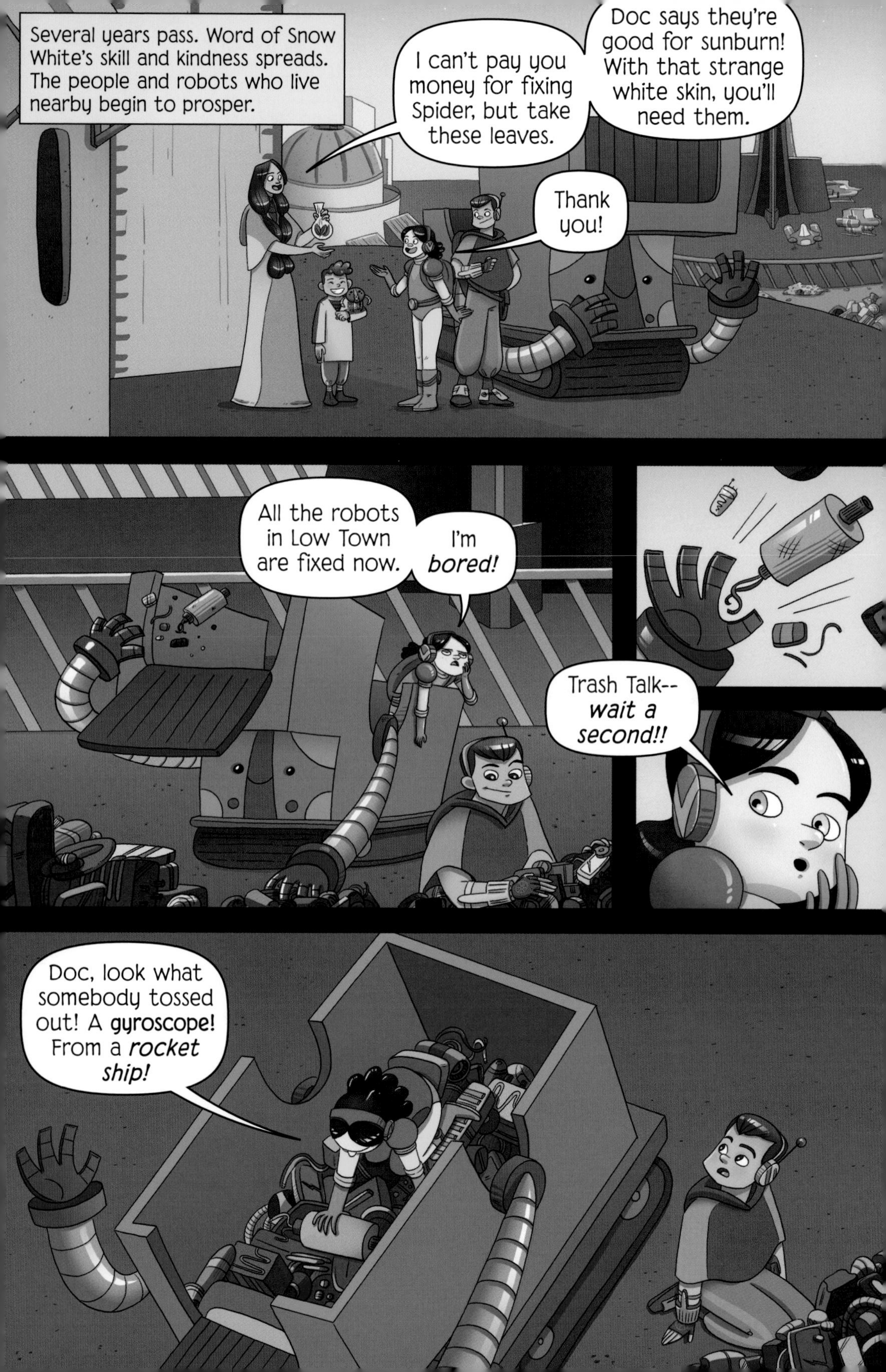
Several years pass. Word of Snow White's skill and kindness spreads. The people and robots who live nearby begin to prosper.
I can't pay you money for fixing Spider, but take these leaves.
Doc says they're good for sunburn! With that strange white skin, you'll need them.
Thank you!
All the robots in Low Town are fixed now.
I'm *bored!*
Trash Talk-- *wait a second!!*
Doc, look what somebody tossed out! A **gyroscope!** From a *rocket ship!*

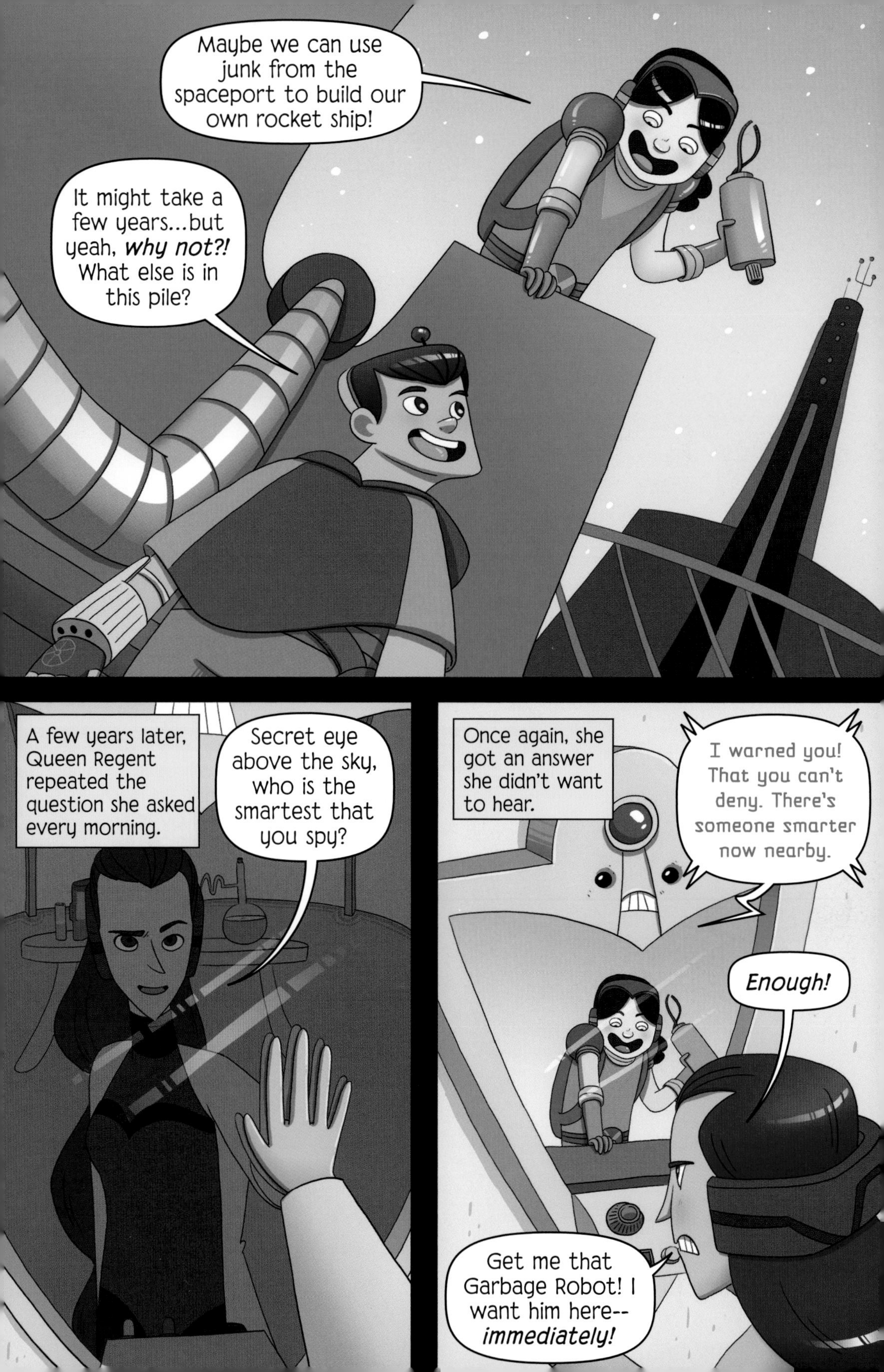
Maybe we can use junk from the spaceport to build our own rocket ship!
It might take a few years...but yeah, *why not?!* What else is in this pile?
A few years later, Queen Regent repeated the question she asked every morning.
Secret eye above the sky, who is the smartest that you spy?
Once again, she got an answer she didn't want to hear.
I warned you! That you can't deny. There's someone smarter now nearby.
Enough!
Get me that Garbage Robot! I want him here-- *immediately!*

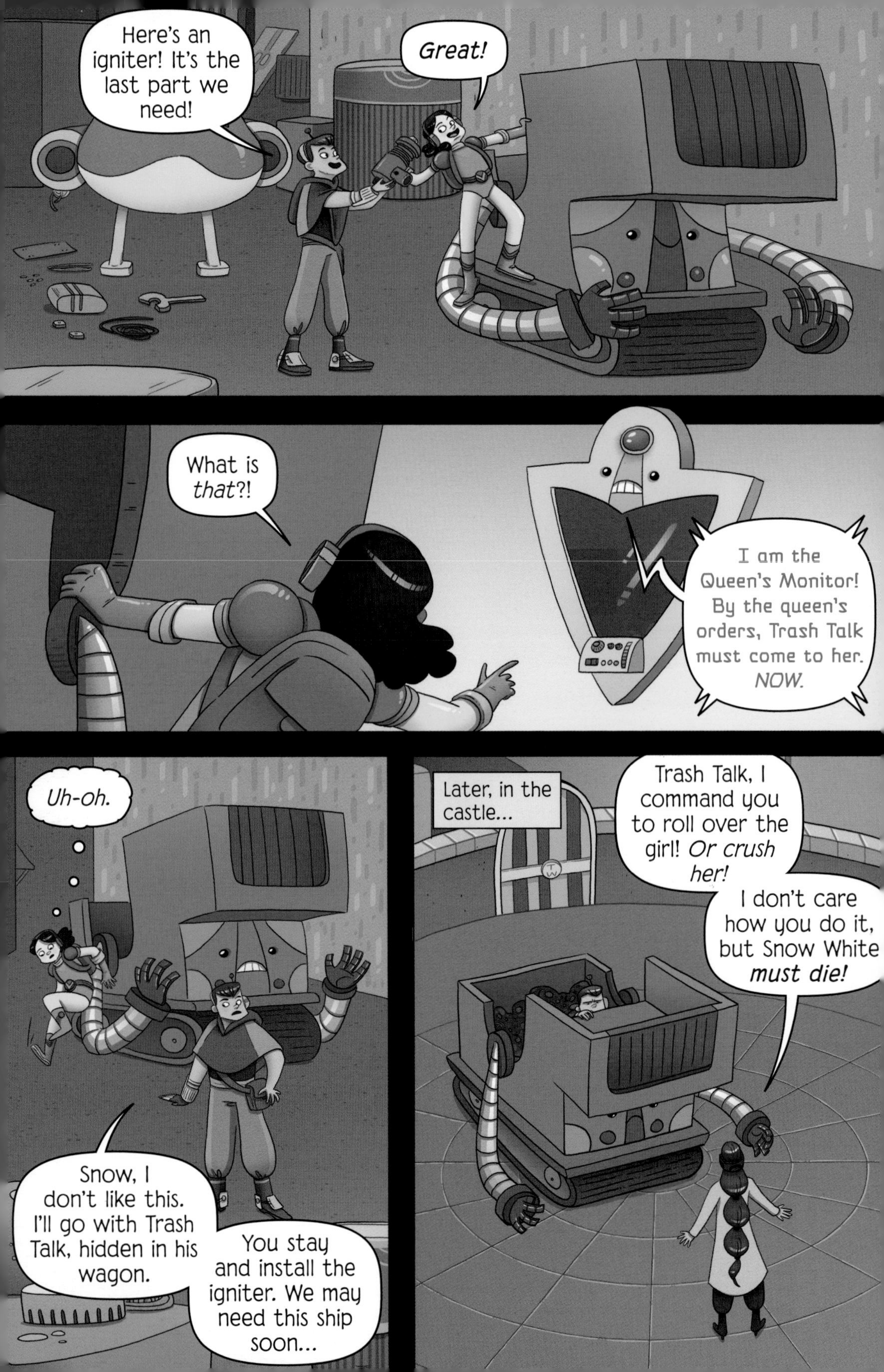

Here's an igniter! It's the last part we need!
Great!
What is *that*?!
I am the Queen's Monitor! By the queen's orders, Trash Talk must come to her. *NOW.*
Uh-oh.
Snow, I don't like this. I'll go with Trash Talk, hidden in his wagon.
You stay and install the igniter. We may need this ship soon...
Later, in the castle...
Trash Talk, I command you to roll over the girl! *Or crush her!*
I don't care how you do it, but Snow White *must die!*

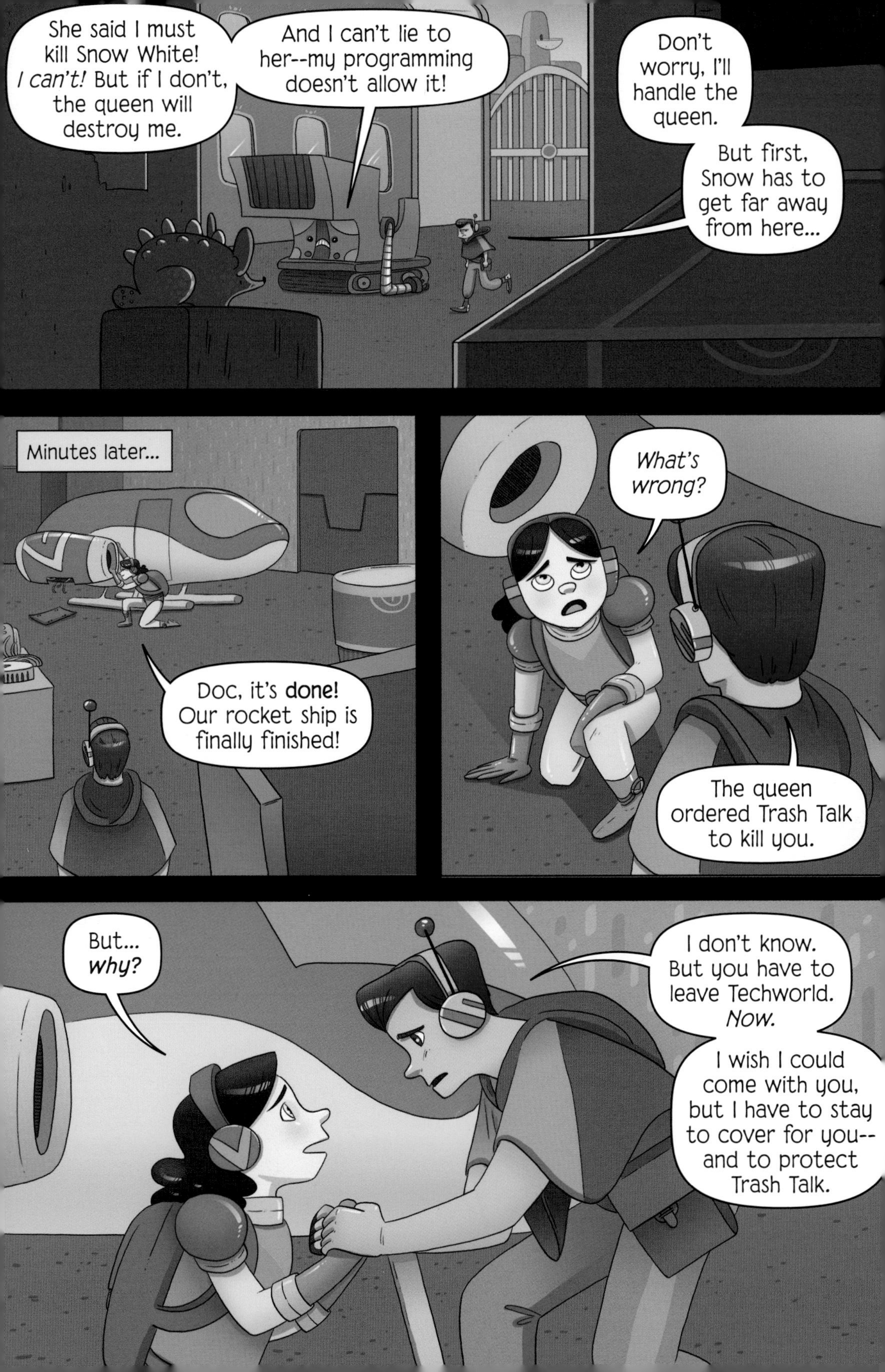
She said I must kill Snow White! *I can't!* But if I don't, the queen will destroy me.
And I can't lie to her--my programming doesn't allow it!
Don't worry, I'll handle the queen.
But first, Snow has to get far away from here...
Minutes later...
Doc, it's **done!** Our rocket ship is finally finished!
What's wrong?
The queen ordered Trash Talk to kill you.
But... *why?*
I don't know. But you have to leave Techworld. *Now.*
I wish I could come with you, but I have to stay to cover for you--and to protect Trash Talk.

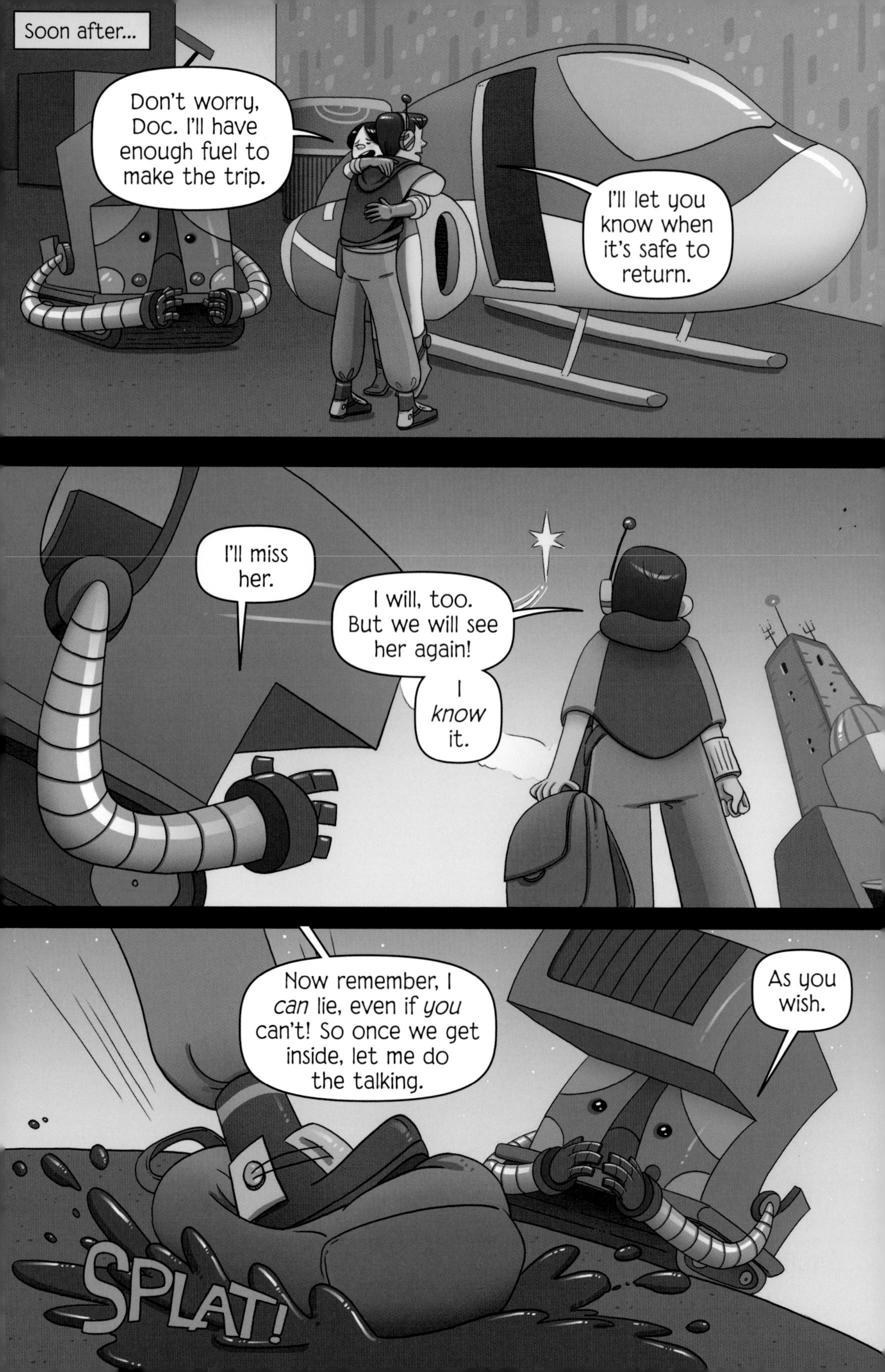
Soon after...
Don't worry, Doc. I'll have enough fuel to make the trip.
I'll let you know when it's safe to return.
I'll miss her.
I will, too. But we will see her again!
I *know* it.
Now remember, I *can* lie, even if *you* can't! So once we get inside, let me do the talking.
As you wish.
SPLAT!

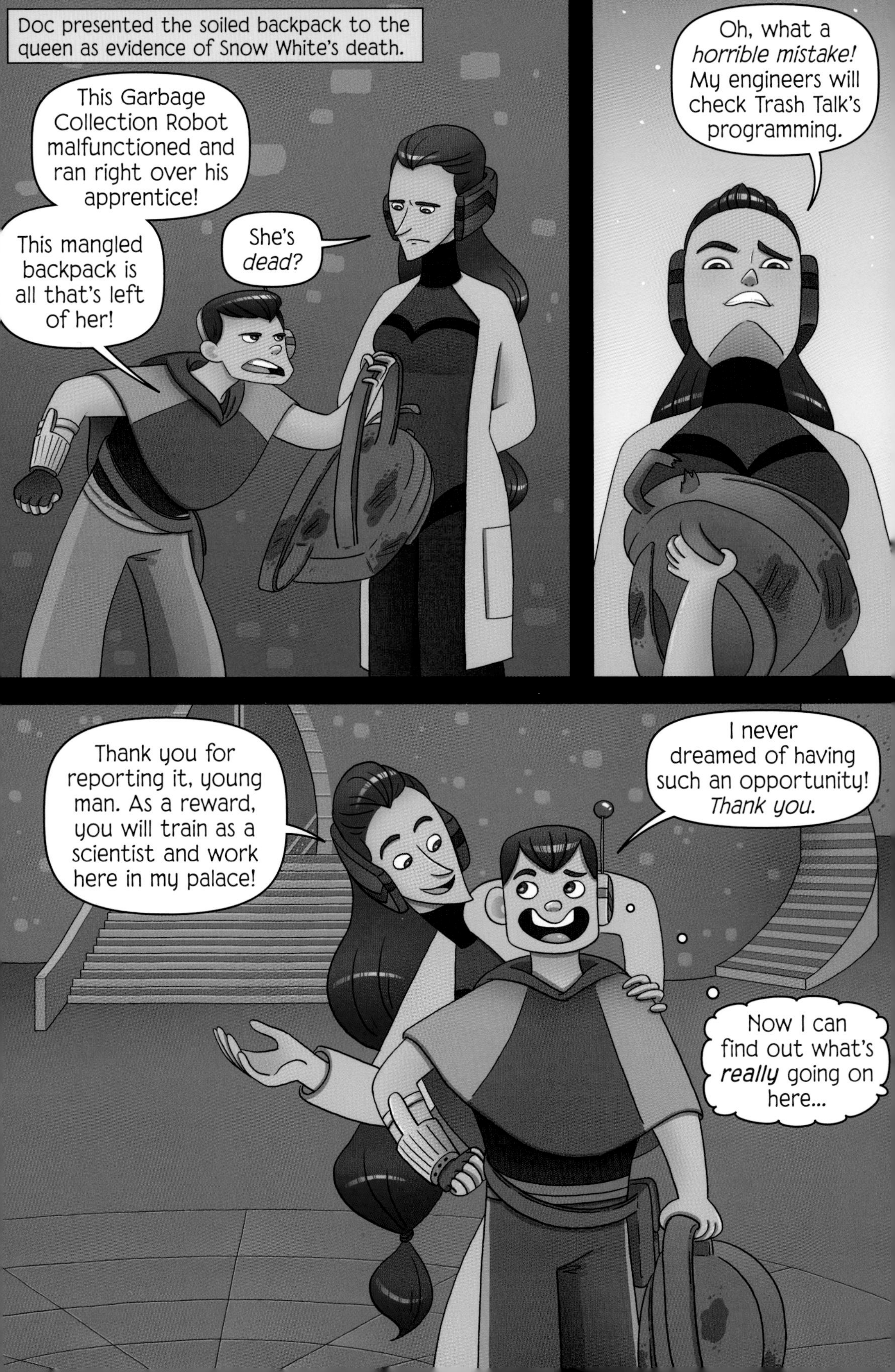
Doc presented the soiled backpack to the queen as evidence of Snow White's death.
This Garbage Collection Robot malfunctioned and ran right over his apprentice!
This mangled backpack is all that's left of her!
She's *dead?*
Oh, what a *horrible mistake!* My engineers will check Trash Talk's programming.
Thank you for reporting it, young man. As a reward, you will train as a scientist and work here in my palace!
I never dreamed of having such an opportunity! *Thank you.*
Now I can find out what's *really* going on here...

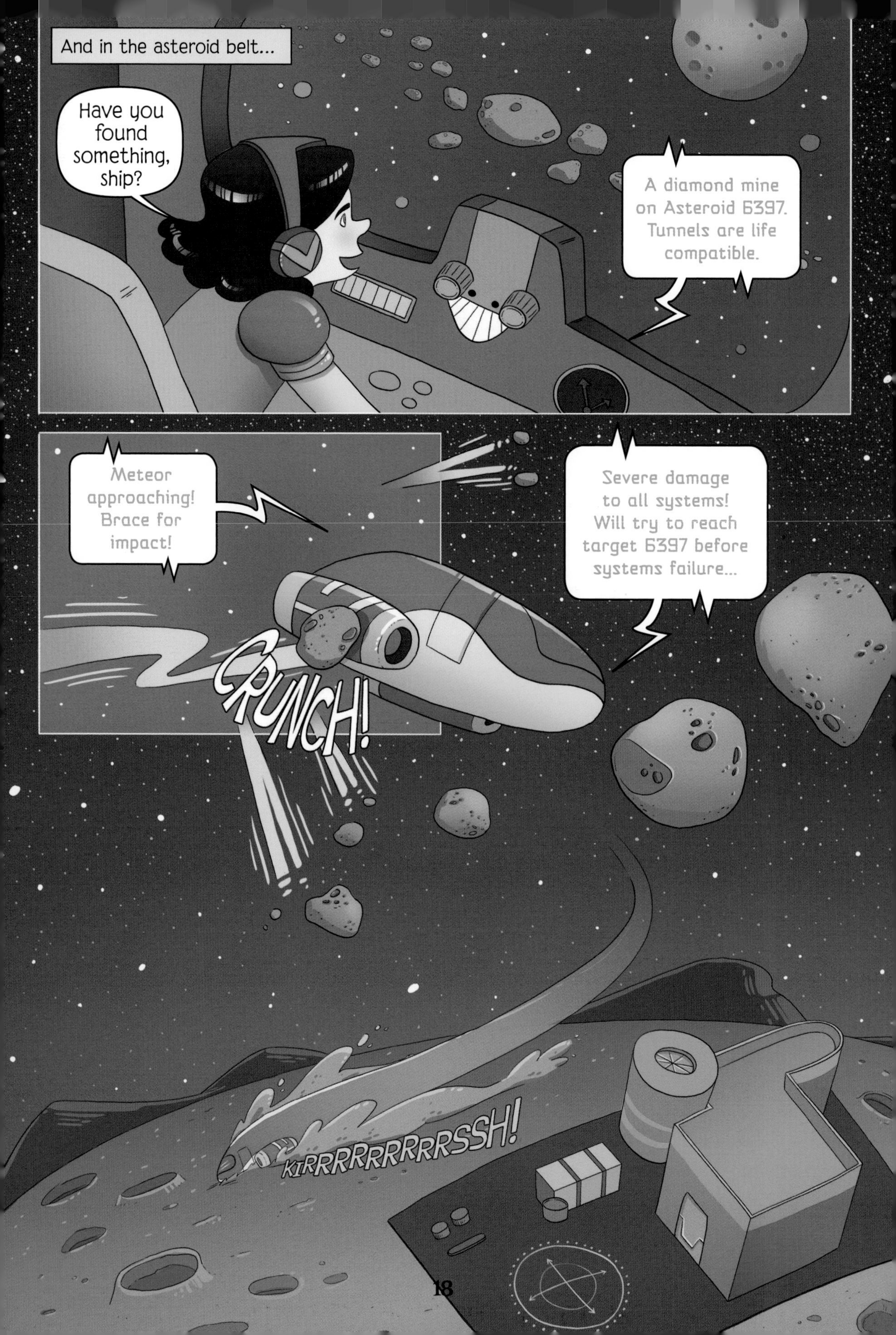
And in the asteroid belt...
Have you found something, ship?
A diamond mine on Asteroid 6397. Tunnels are life compatible.
Meteor approaching! Brace for impact!
CRUNCH!
Severe damage to all systems! Will try to reach target 6397 before systems failure...
KIRRRRRRRRRRSSH!

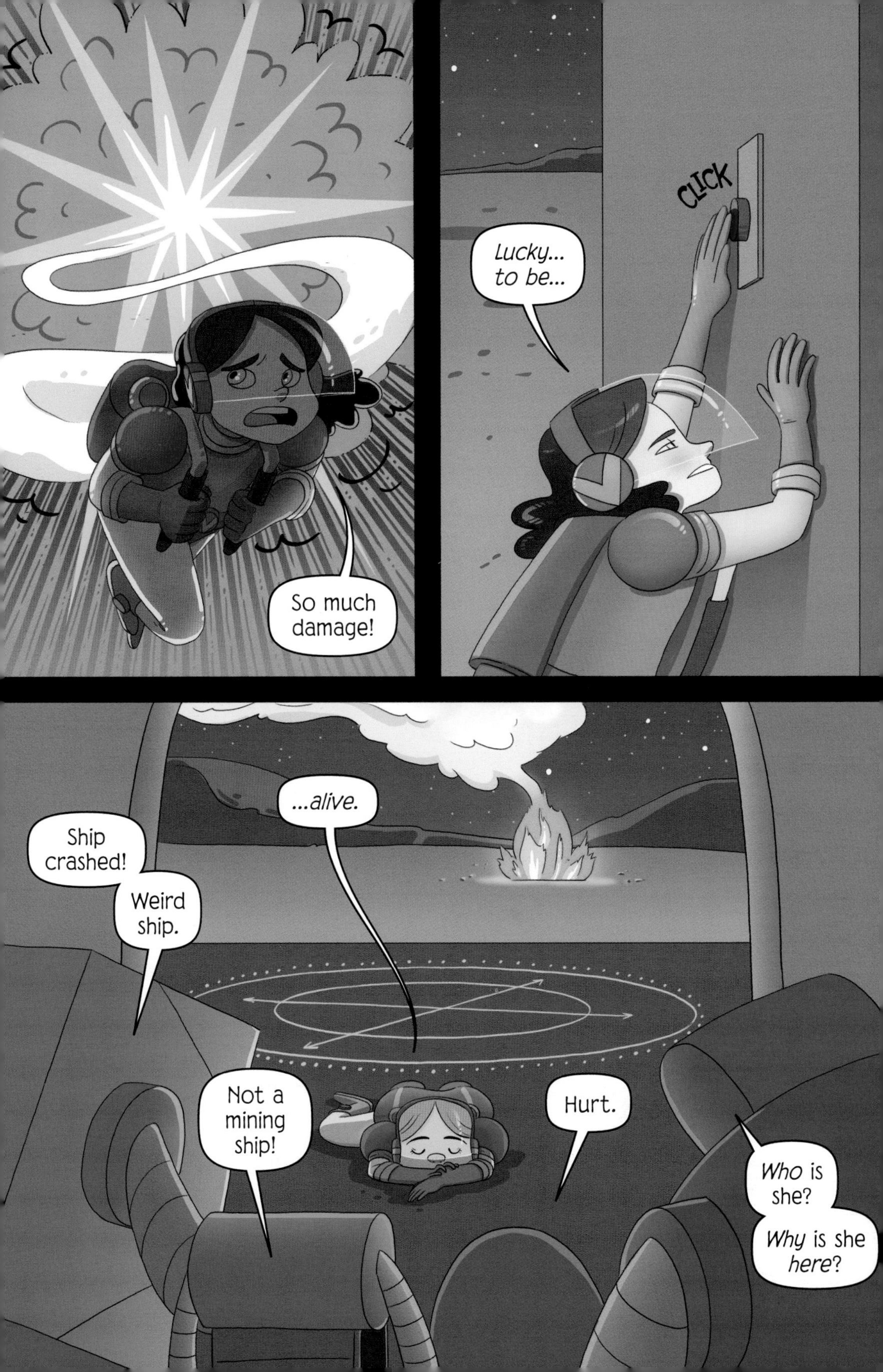
So much damage!
CLICK
Lucky... to be...
...alive.
Ship crashed!
Weird ship.
Not a mining ship!
Hurt.
Who is she?
Why is she here?

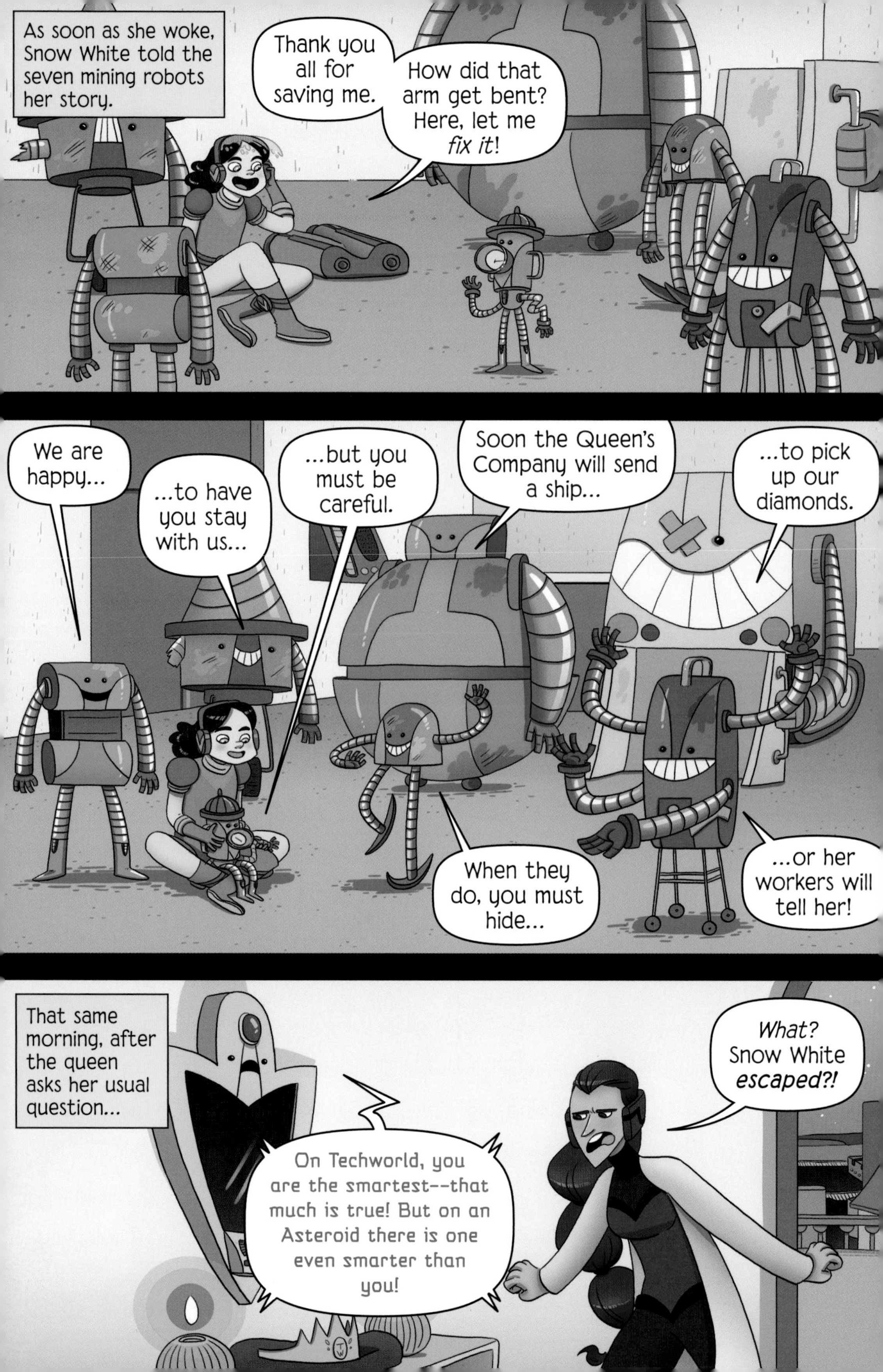

As soon as she woke, Snow White told the seven mining robots her story.
Thank you all for saving me.
How did that arm get bent? Here, let me *fix it*!
We are happy...
...to have you stay with us...
...but you must be careful.
Soon the Queen's Company will send a ship...
...to pick up our diamonds.
When they do, you must hide...
...or her workers will tell her!
That same morning, after the queen asks her usual question...
On Techworld, you are the smartest--that much is true! But on an Asteroid there is one even smarter than you!
What? Snow White *escaped?!*

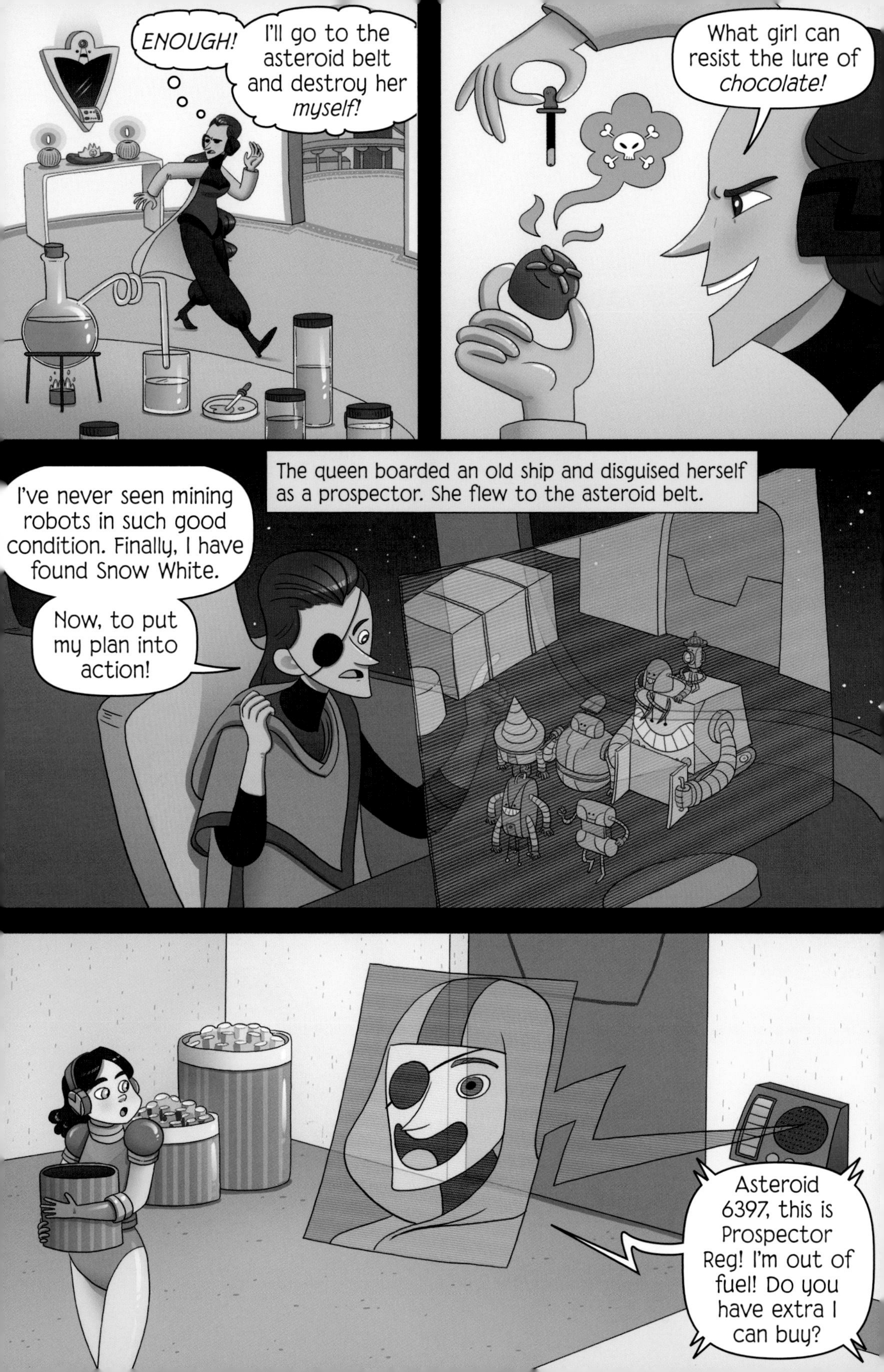
ENOUGH!
I'll go to the asteroid belt and destroy her *myself!*
What girl can resist the lure of *chocolate!*
The queen boarded an old ship and disguised herself as a prospector. She flew to the asteroid belt.
I've never seen mining robots in such good condition. Finally, I have found Snow White.
Now, to put my plan into action!
Asteroid 6397, this is Prospector Reg! I'm out of fuel! Do you have extra I can buy?

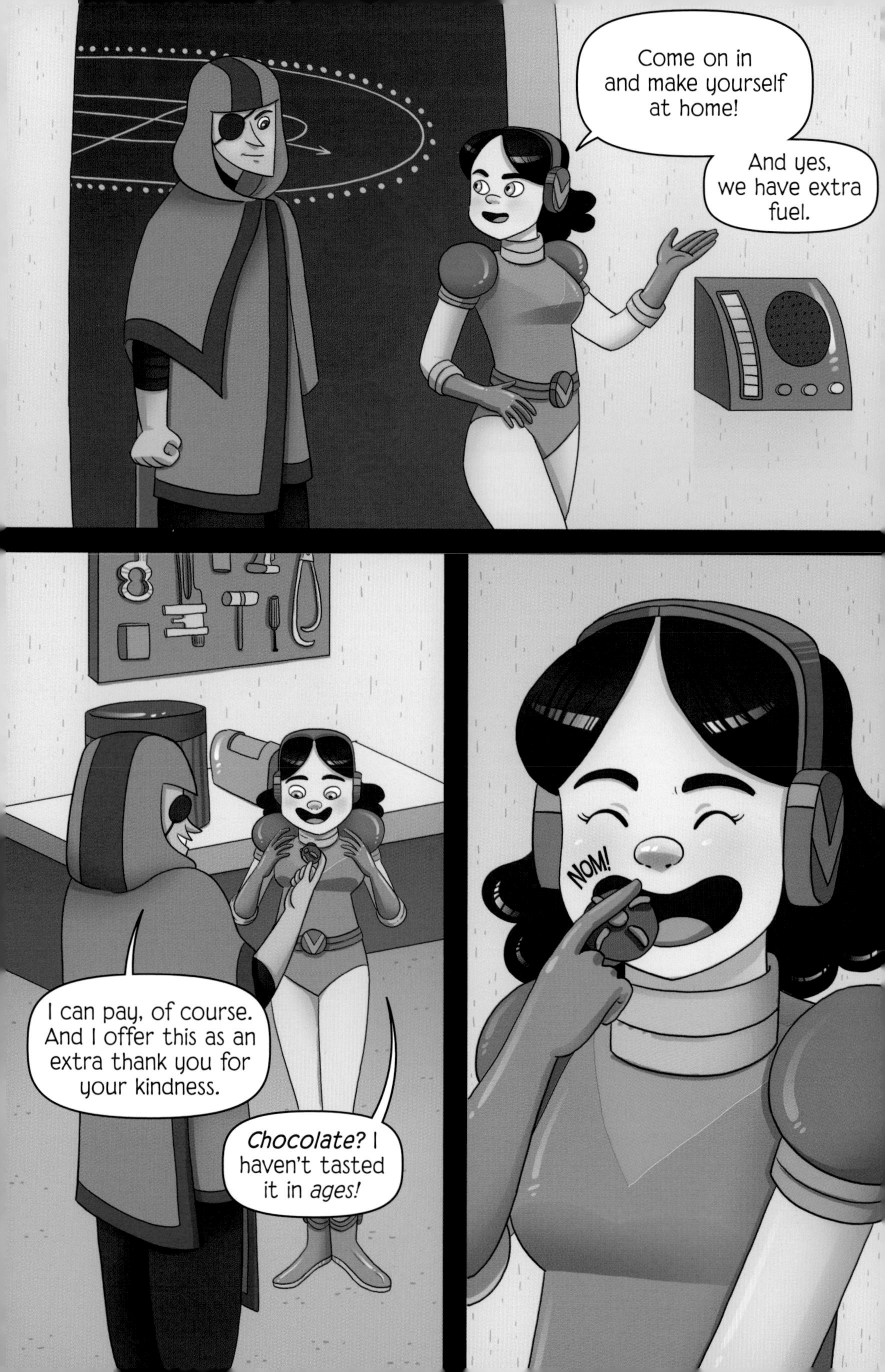
Come on in and make yourself at home!
And yes, we have extra fuel.
I can pay, of course. And I offer this as an extra thank you for your kindness.
Chocolate? I haven't tasted it in *ages!*
NOM!

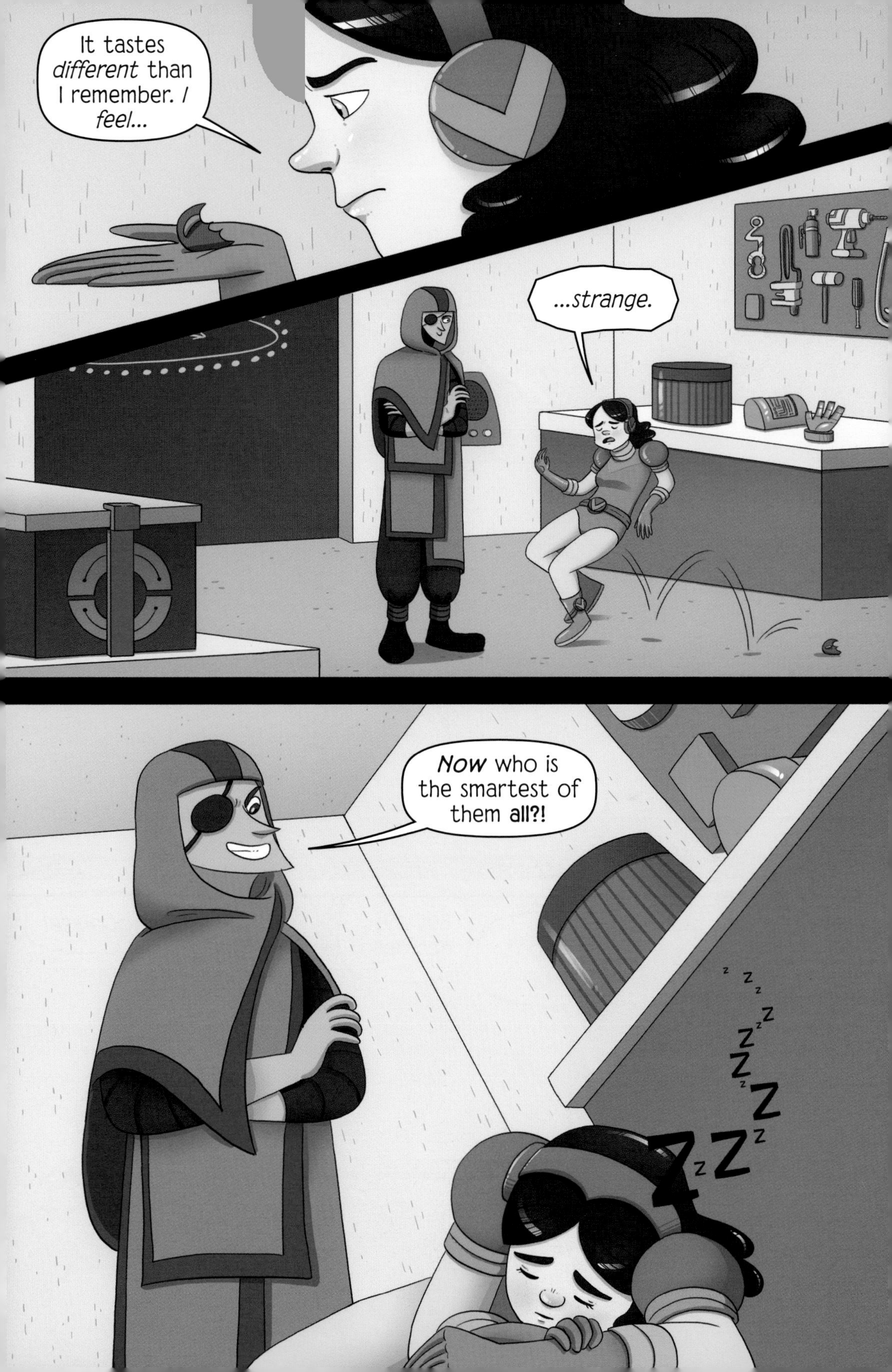
It tastes *different* than I remember. *I feel...*
...strange.
Now who is the smartest of them **all?!**
Z Z Z Z Z Z Z Z Z Z Z

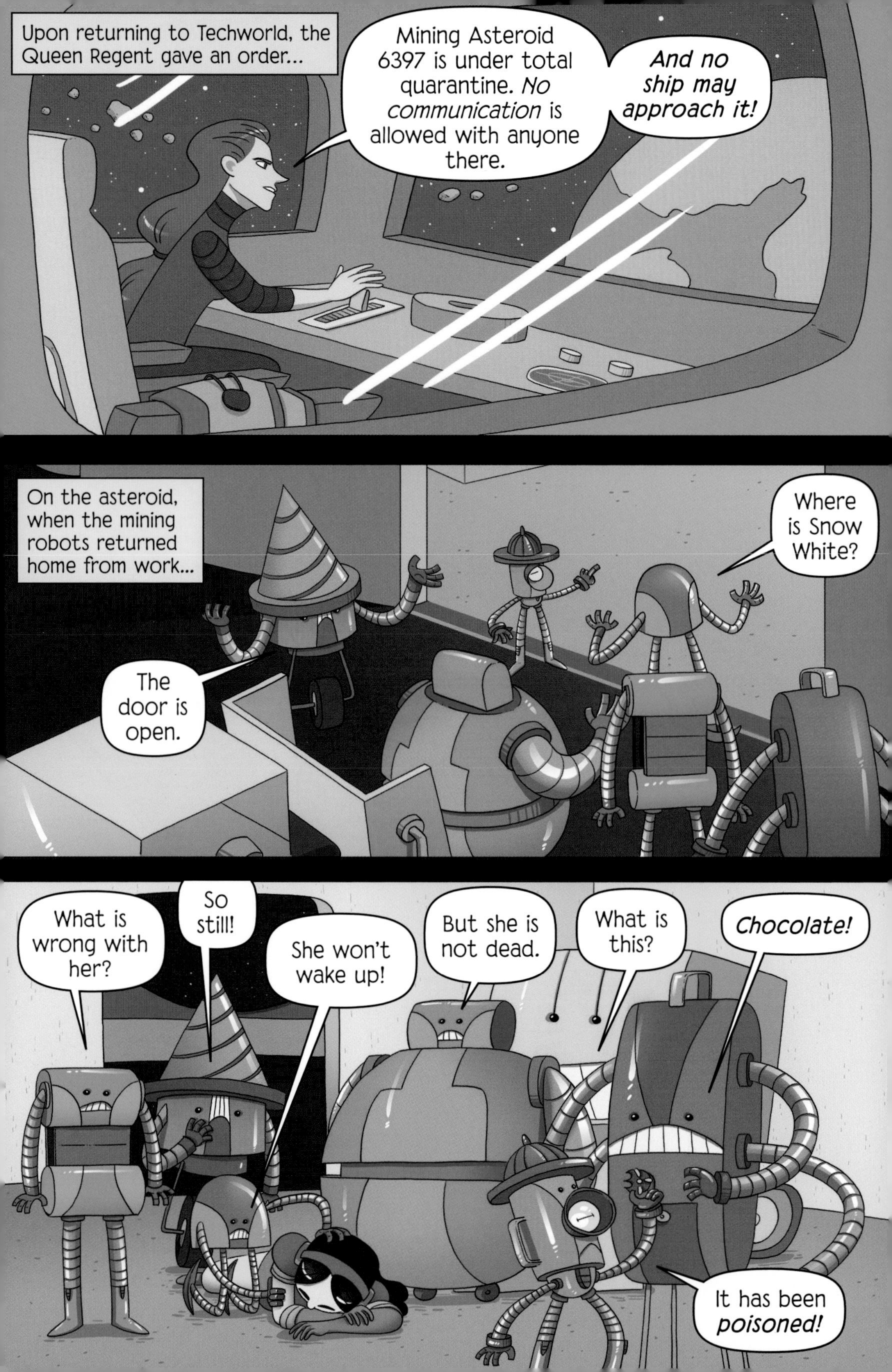

Upon returning to Techworld, the Queen Regent gave an order...
Mining Asteroid 6397 is under total quarantine. *No communication* is allowed with anyone there.
And no ship may approach it!
On the asteroid, when the mining robots returned home from work...
Where is Snow White?
The door is open.
What is wrong with her?
So still!
She won't wake up!
But she is not dead.
What is this?
Chocolate!
It has been *poisoned!*

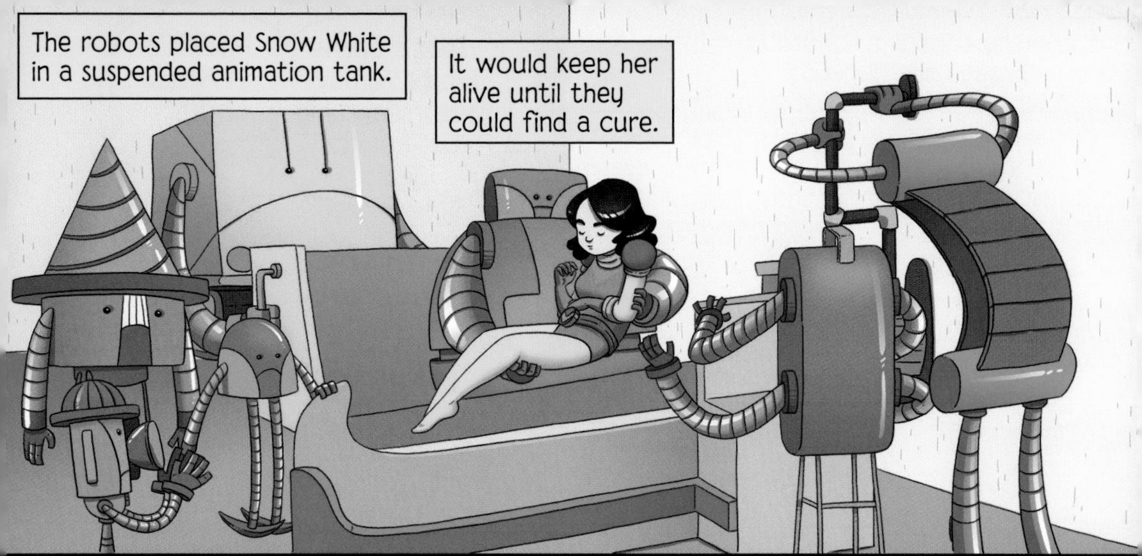
The robots placed Snow White in a suspended animation tank.
It would keep her alive until they could find a cure.

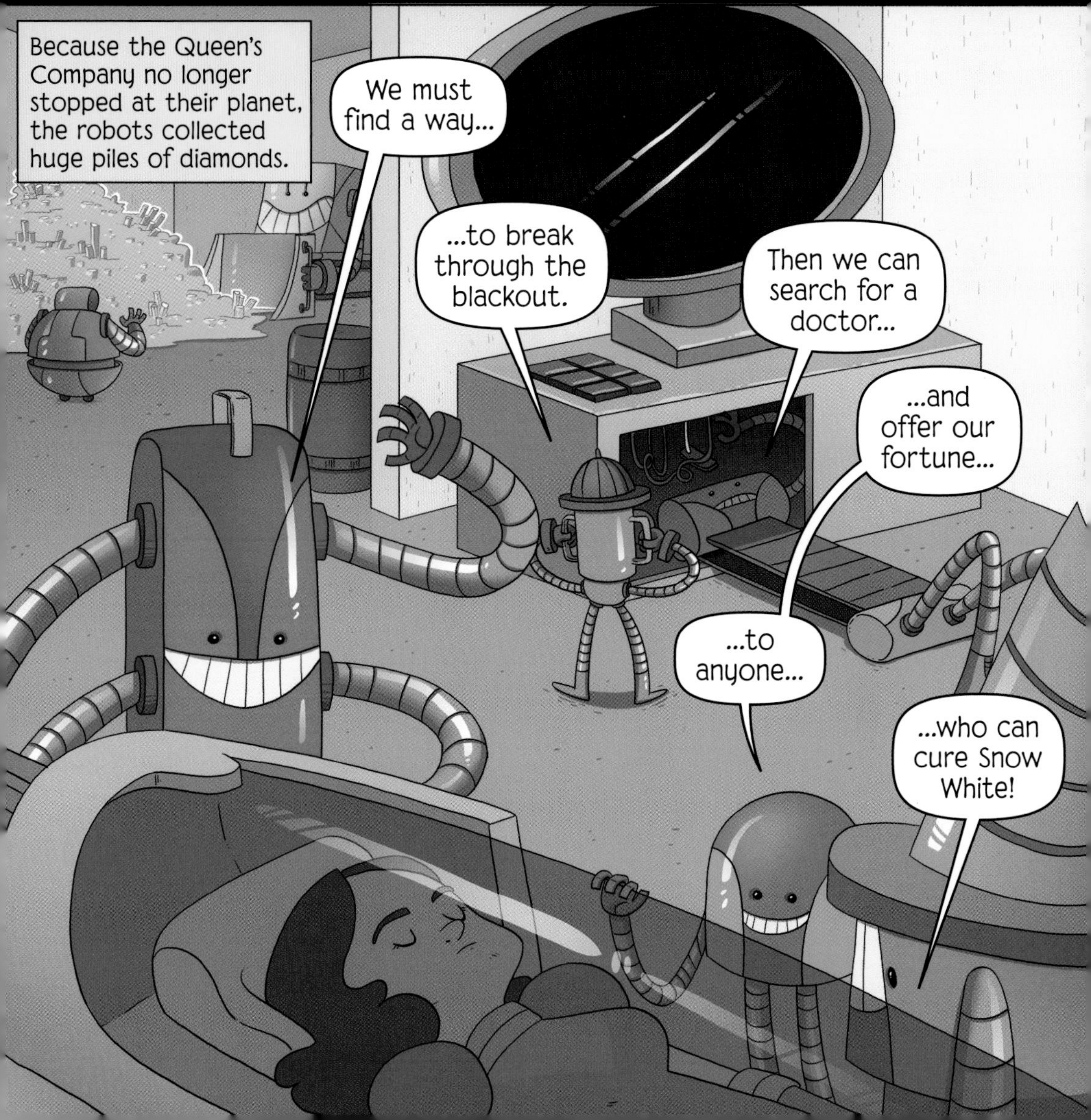
Because the Queen's Company no longer stopped at their planet, the robots collected huge piles of diamonds.
We must find a way...
...to break through the blackout.
Then we can search for a doctor...
...and offer our fortune...
...to anyone...
...who can cure Snow White!

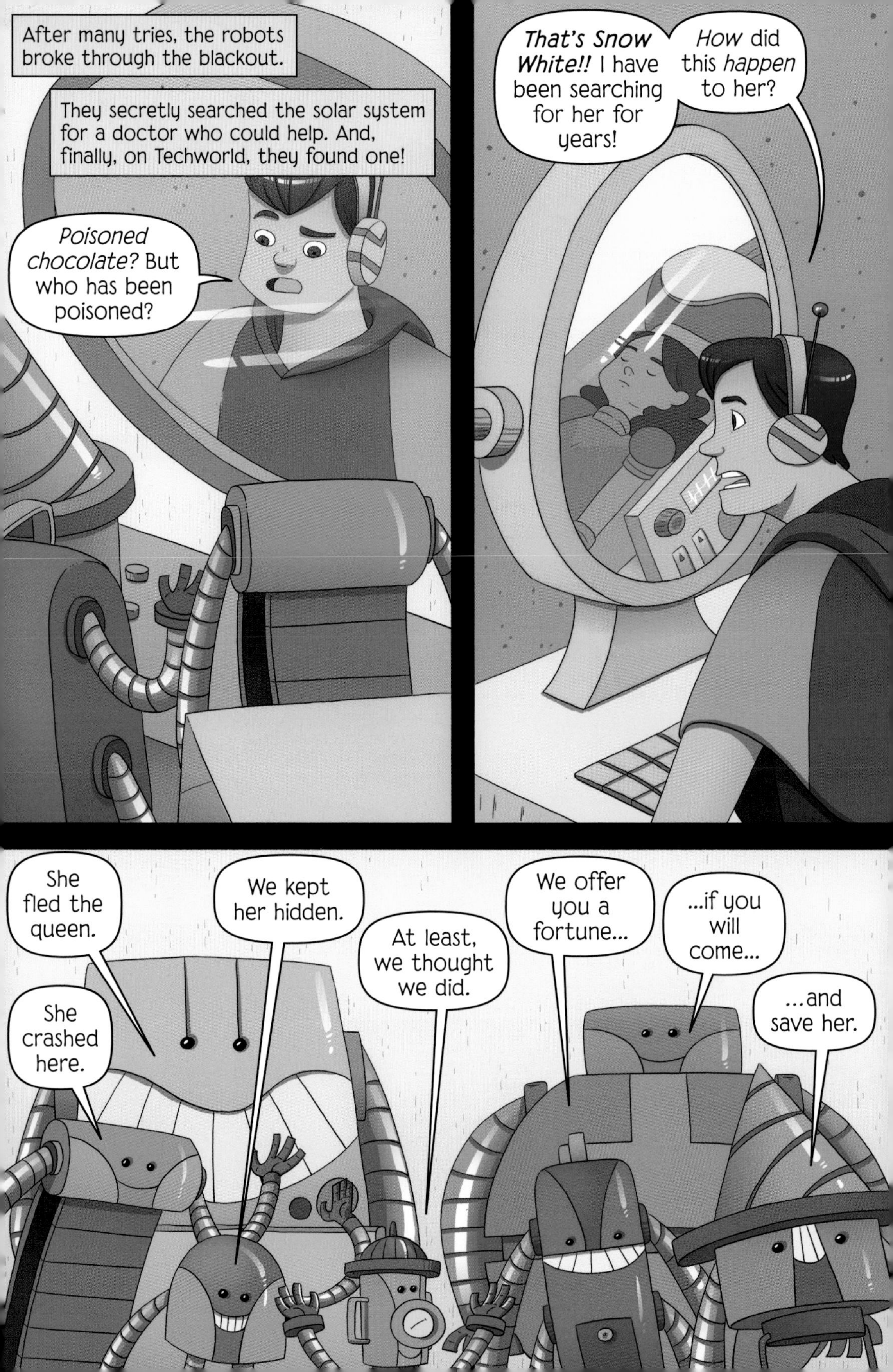
After many tries, the robots broke through the blackout.
They secretly searched the solar system for a doctor who could help. And, finally, on Techworld, they found one!
Poisoned chocolate? But who has been poisoned?
That's Snow White!! I have been searching for her for years!
How did this *happen* to her?
She fled the queen.
She crashed here.
We kept her hidden.
At least, we thought we did.
We offer you a fortune...
...if you will come...
...and save her.

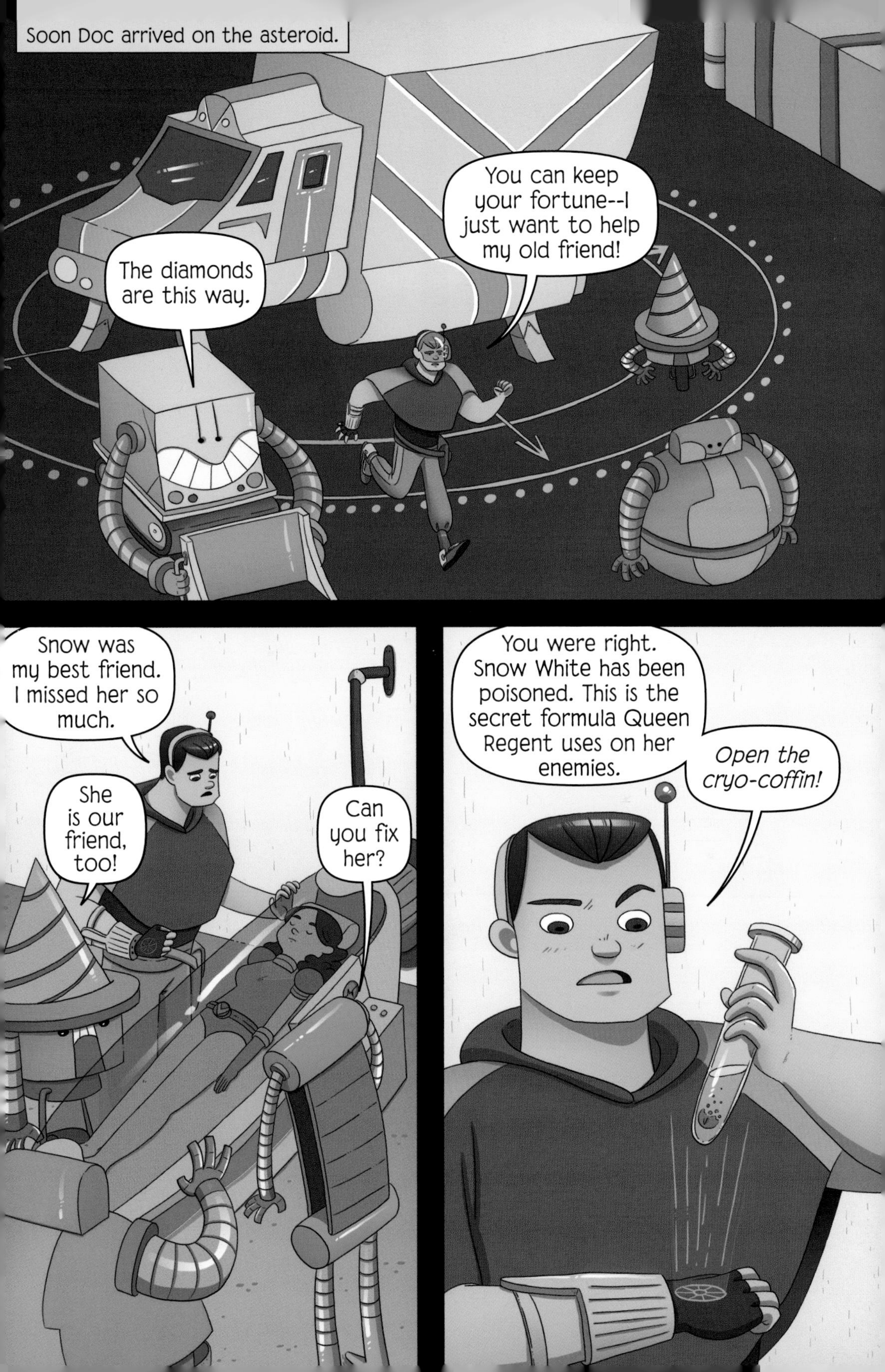
Soon Doc arrived on the asteroid.
The diamonds are this way.
You can keep your fortune--I just want to help my old friend!
Snow was my best friend. I missed her so much.
She is our friend, too!
Can you fix her?
You were right. Snow White has been poisoned. This is the secret formula Queen Regent uses on her enemies.
Open the cryo-coffin!

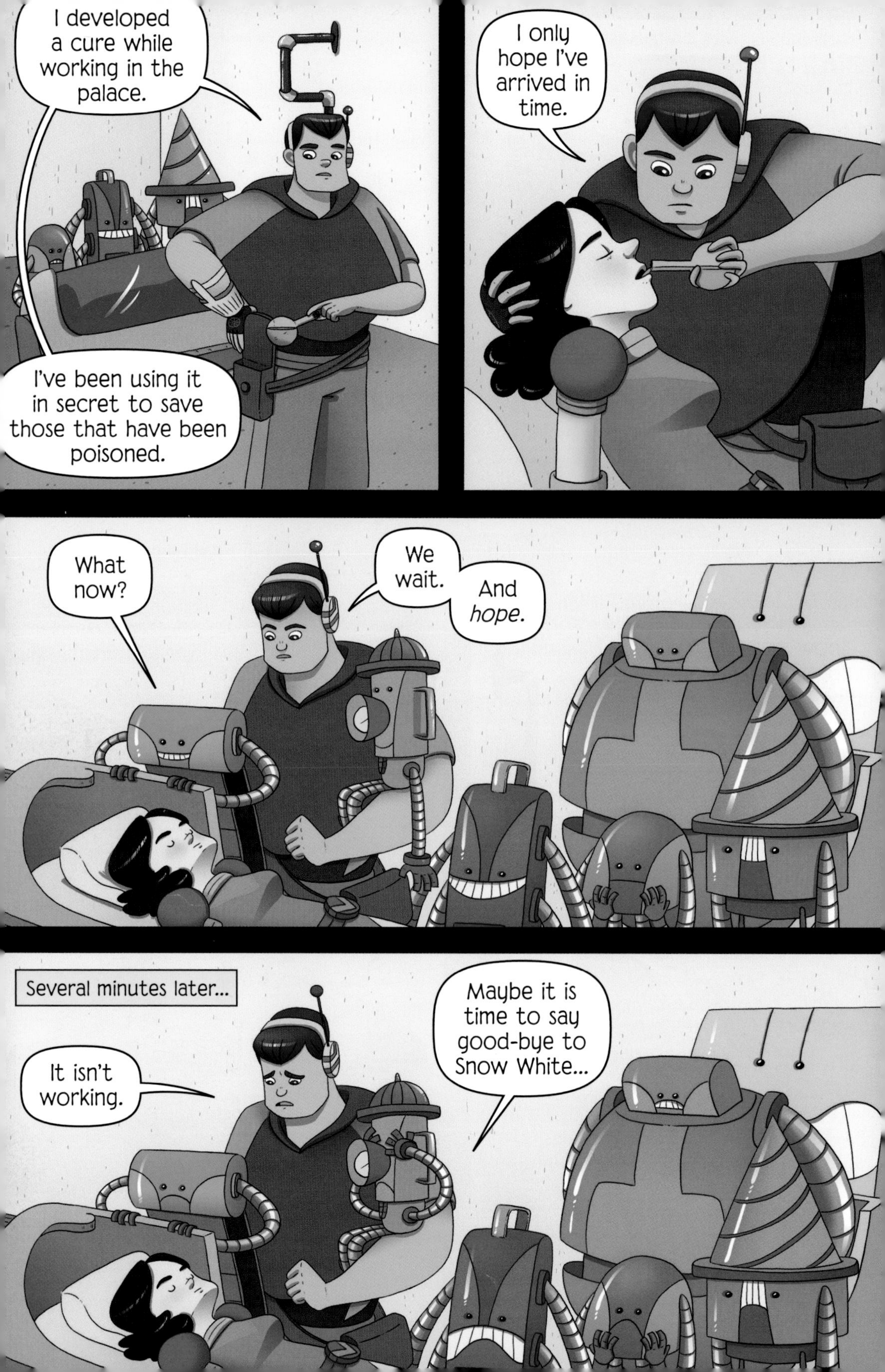
I developed a cure while working in the palace.
I've been using it in secret to save those that have been poisoned.
I only hope I've arrived in time.
What now?
We wait.
And *hope*.
Several minutes later...
It isn't working.
Maybe it is time to say good-bye to Snow White...

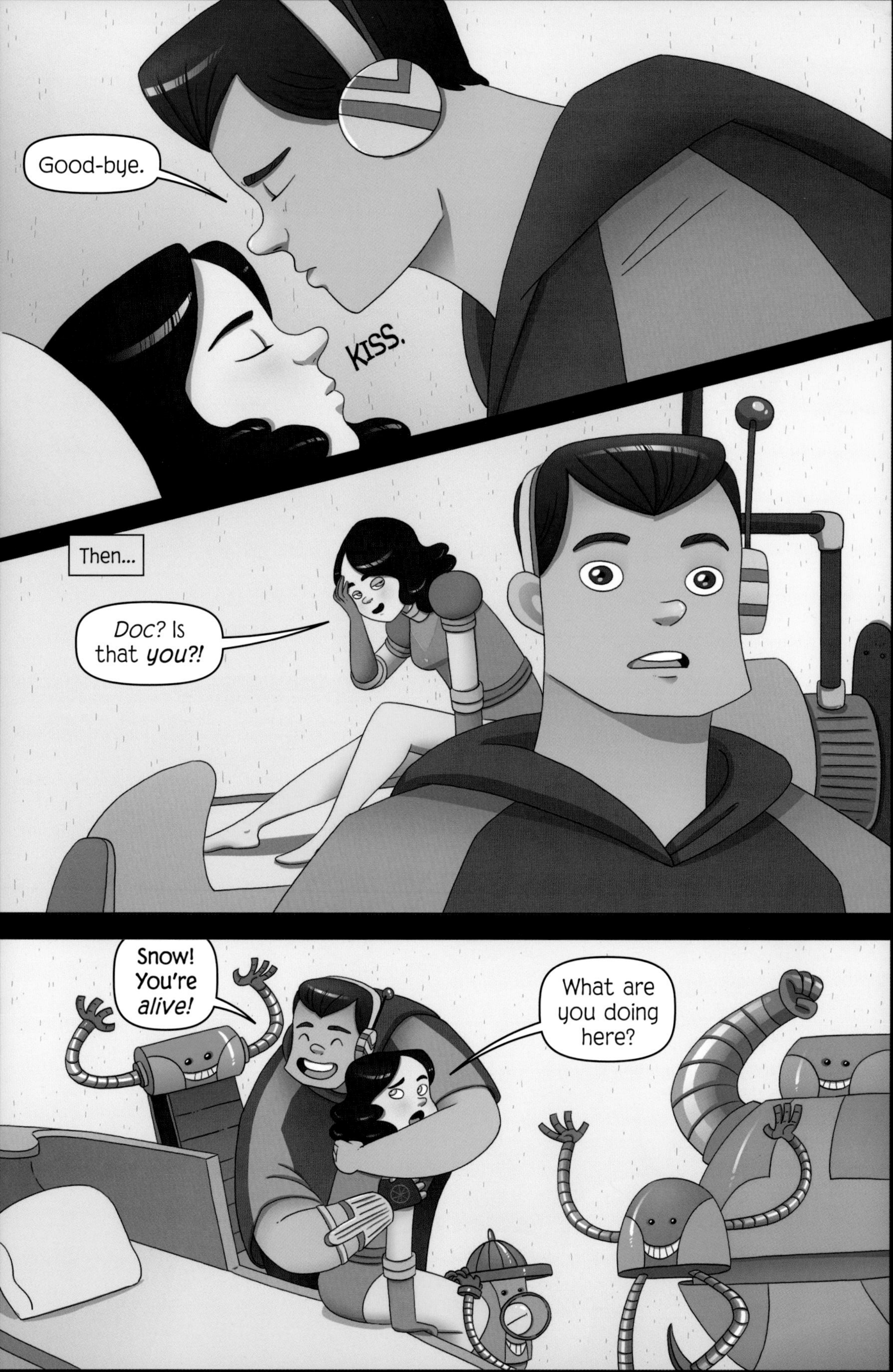
Good-bye.
KISS.
Then...
Doc? Is that ***you?!***
Snow! ***You're*** *alive!*
What are you doing here?

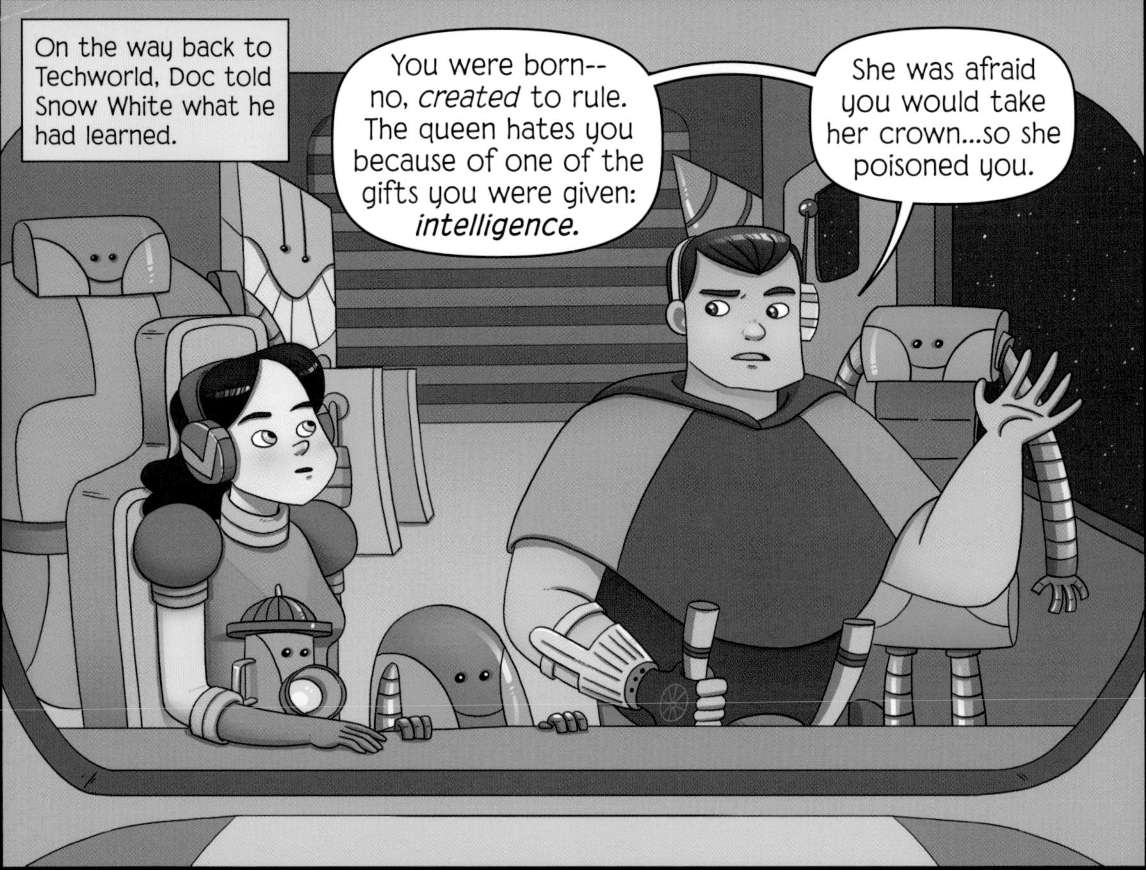
On the way back to Techworld, Doc told Snow White what he had learned.
You were born--no, *created* to rule. The queen hates you because of one of the gifts you were given: ***intelligence.***
She was afraid you would take her crown...so she poisoned you.

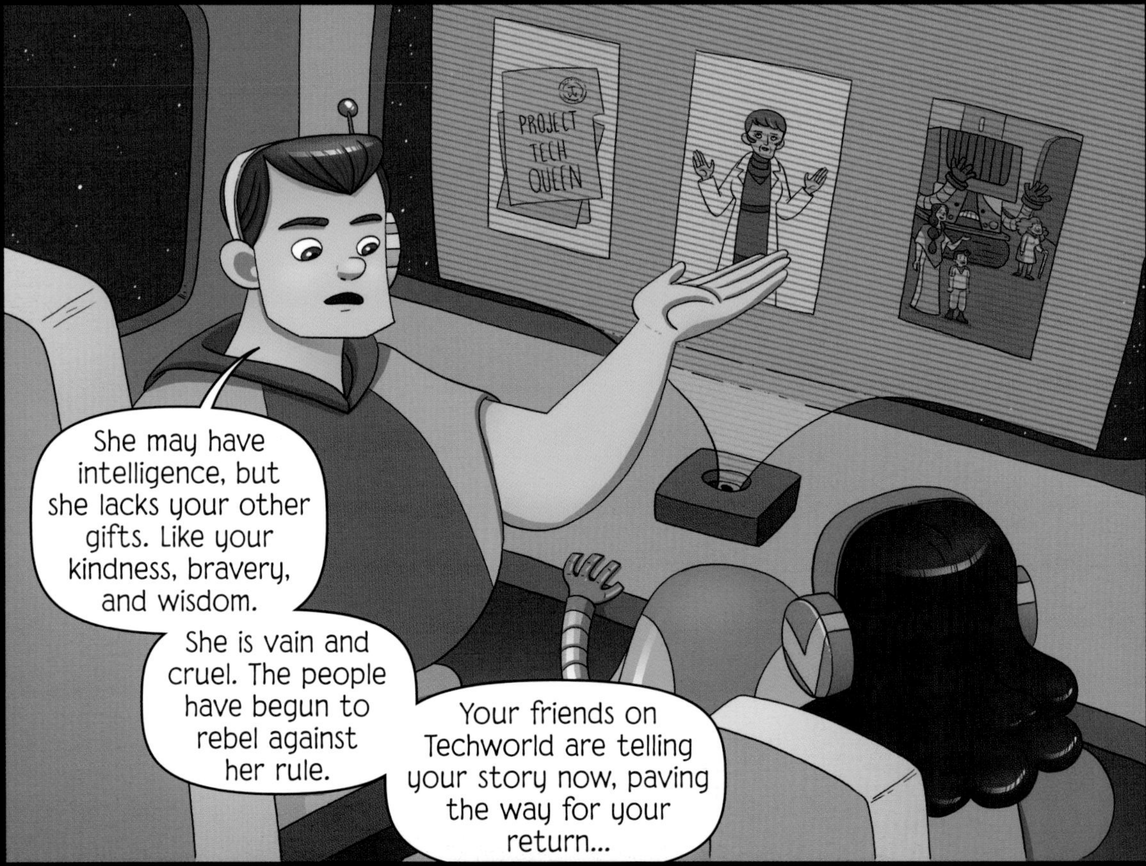
PROJECT TECH QUEEN
She may have intelligence, but she lacks your other gifts. Like your kindness, bravery, and wisdom.
She is vain and cruel. The people have begun to rebel against her rule.
Your friends on Techworld are telling your story now, paving the way for your return...

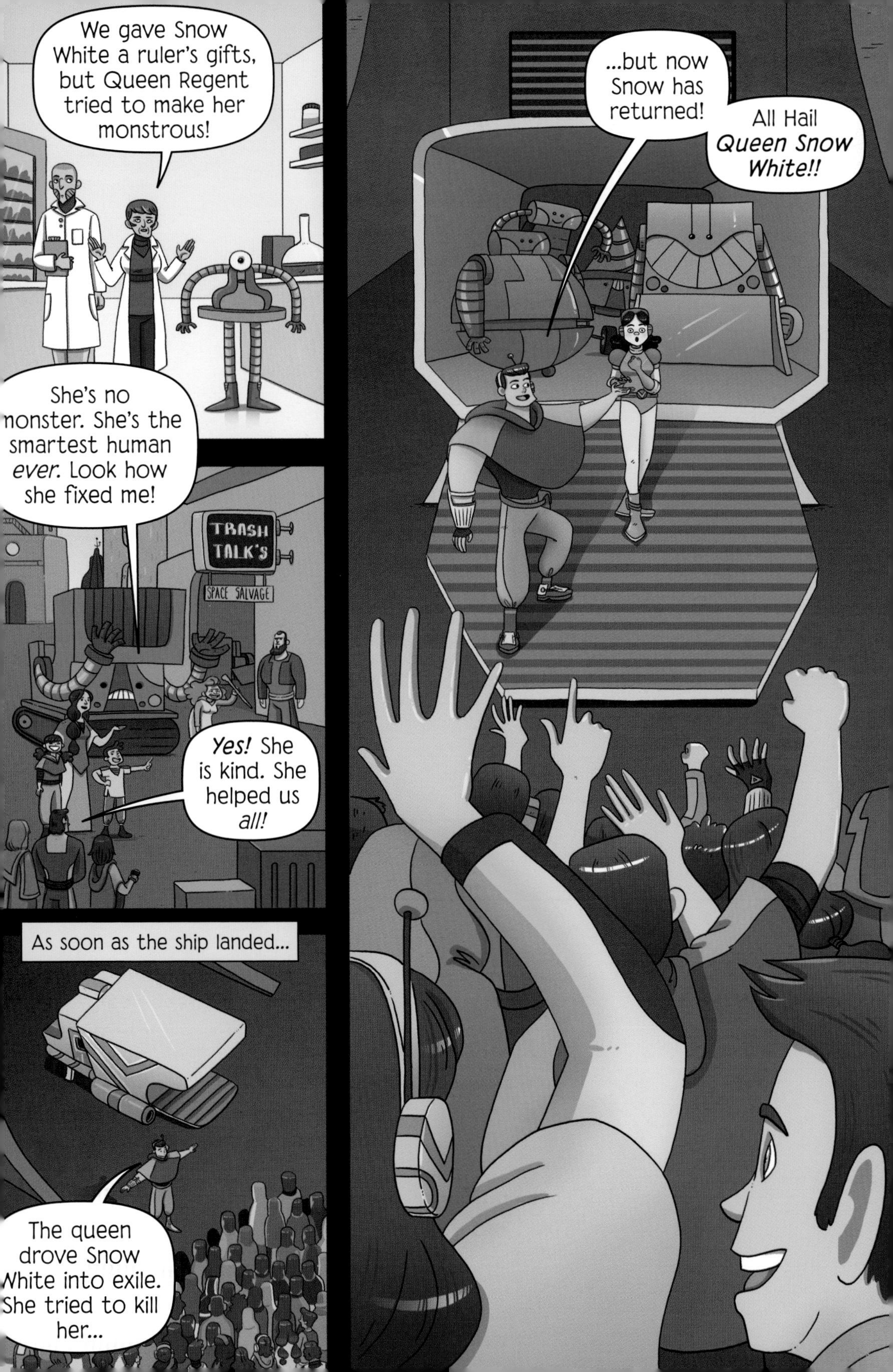
We gave Snow White a ruler's gifts, but Queen Regent tried to make her monstrous!
She's no monster. She's the smartest human *ever.* Look how she fixed me!
TRASH TALK'S
SPACE SALVAGE
Yes! She is kind. She helped us *all!*
As soon as the ship landed...
The queen drove Snow White into exile. She tried to kill her...
...but now Snow has returned!
All Hail *Queen Snow White!!*

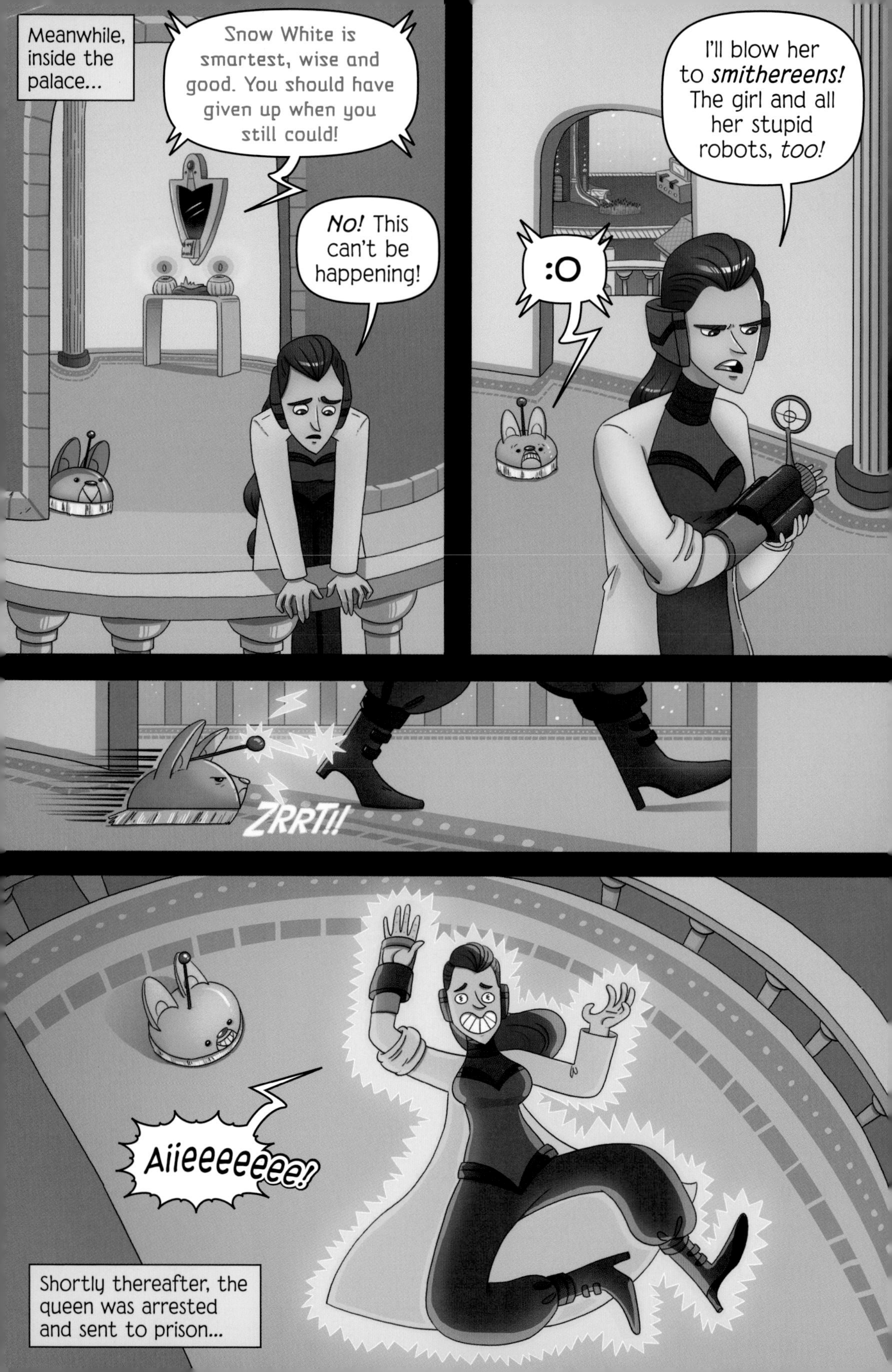
Meanwhile, inside the palace...
Snow White is smartest, wise and good. You should have given up when you still could!
No! This can't be happening!
I'll blow her to ***smithereens!*** The girl and all her stupid robots, *too!*
:O
ZRRT!!
Aiieeeeeeee!
Shortly thereafter, the queen was arrested and sent to prison...

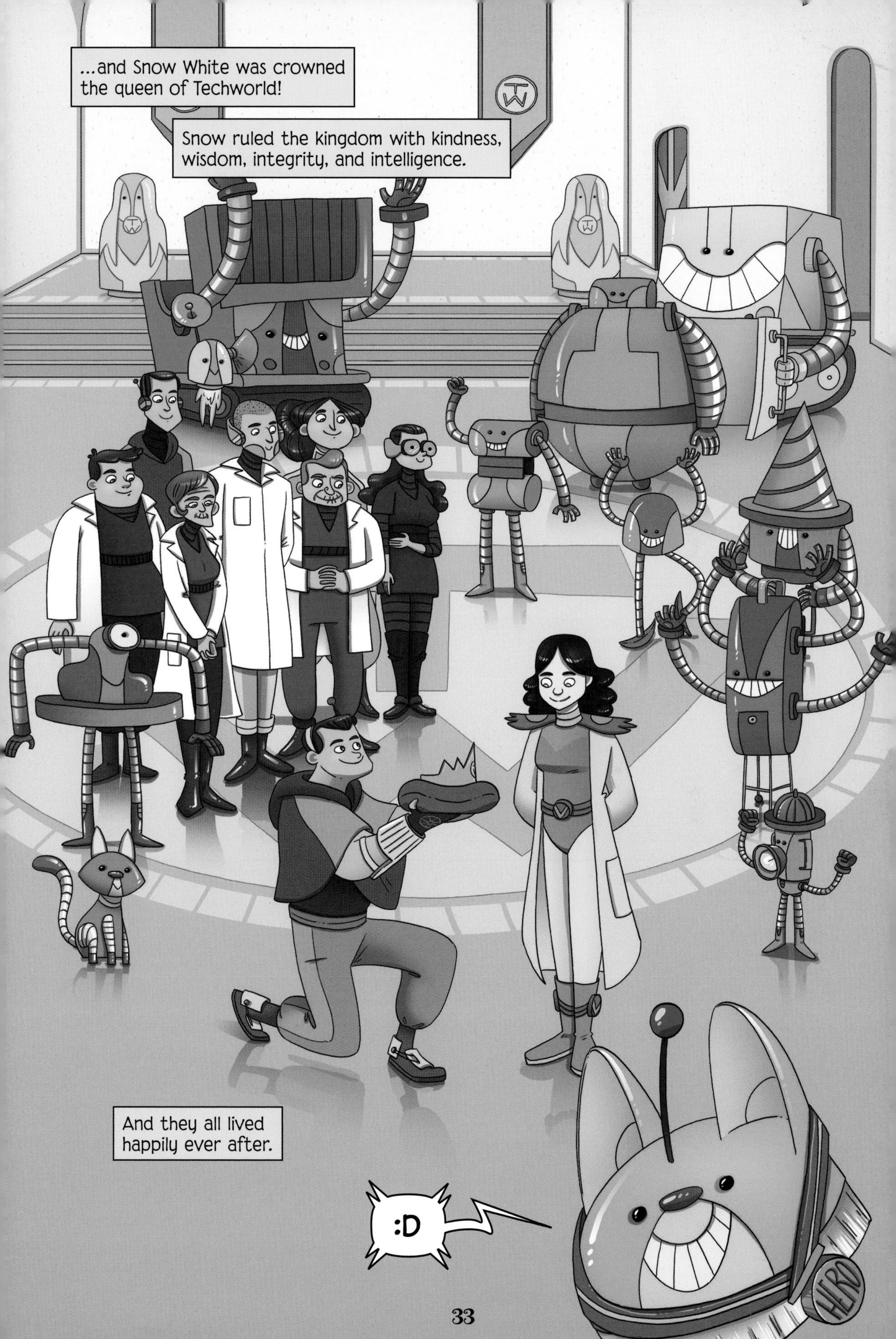
...and Snow White was crowned the queen of Techworld!
Snow ruled the kingdom with kindness, wisdom, integrity, and intelligence.
And they all lived happily ever after.
:D
HERO

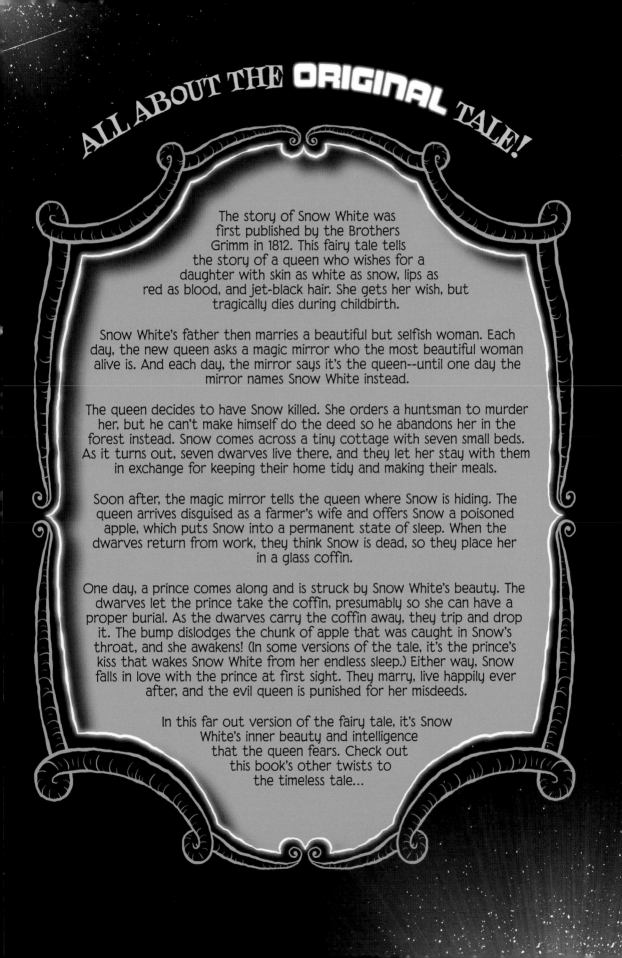

ALL ABOUT THE ORIGINAL TALE!

The story of Snow White was
first published by the Brothers
Grimm in 1812. This fairy tale tells
the story of a queen who wishes for a
daughter with skin as white as snow, lips as
red as blood, and jet-black hair. She gets her wish, but
tragically dies during childbirth.

Snow White's father then marries a beautiful but selfish woman. Each
day, the new queen asks a magic mirror who the most beautiful woman
alive is. And each day, the mirror says it's the queen--until one day the
mirror names Snow White instead.

The queen decides to have Snow killed. She orders a huntsman to murder
her, but he can't make himself do the deed so he abandons her in the
forest instead. Snow comes across a tiny cottage with seven small beds.
As it turns out, seven dwarves live there, and they let her stay with them
in exchange for keeping their home tidy and making their meals.

Soon after, the magic mirror tells the queen where Snow is hiding. The
queen arrives disguised as a farmer's wife and offers Snow a poisoned
apple, which puts Snow into a permanent state of sleep. When the
dwarves return from work, they think Snow is dead, so they place her
in a glass coffin.

One day, a prince comes along and is struck by Snow White's beauty. The
dwarves let the prince take the coffin, presumably so she can have a
proper burial. As the dwarves carry the coffin away, they trip and drop
it. The bump dislodges the chunk of apple that was caught in Snow's
throat, and she awakens! (In some versions of the tale, it's the prince's
kiss that wakes Snow White from her endless sleep.) Either way, Snow
falls in love with the prince at first sight. They marry, live happily ever
after, and the evil queen is punished for her misdeeds.

In this far out version of the fairy tale, it's Snow
White's inner beauty and intelligence
that the queen fears. Check out
this book's other twists to
the timeless tale...

A FAR OUT GUIDE TO SNOW WHITE'S TALE TWISTS!

The all-knowing magic mirror is replaced by an all-seeing space satellite!

Dwarves helped the original Snow White. In this tale, robots come to her aid!

Instead of a poisoned apple putting Snow to sleep, poisoned chocolate is the culprit.

This cryo-tank preserves Snow White instead of the glass coffin in the original tale.

VISUAL QUESTIONS

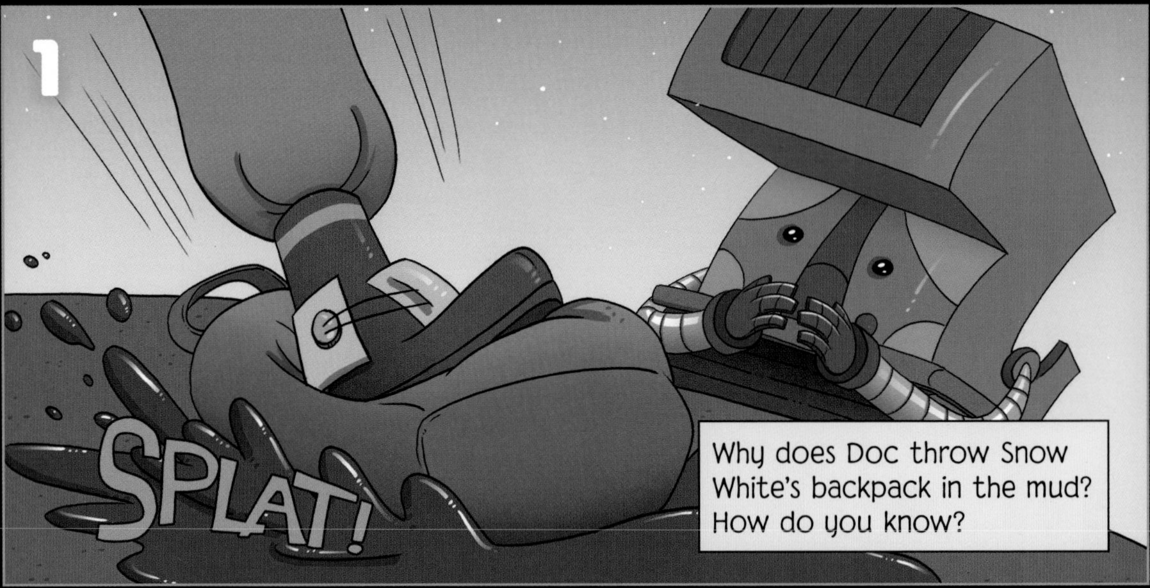
1
SPLAT!
Why does Doc throw Snow White's backpack in the mud? How do you know?

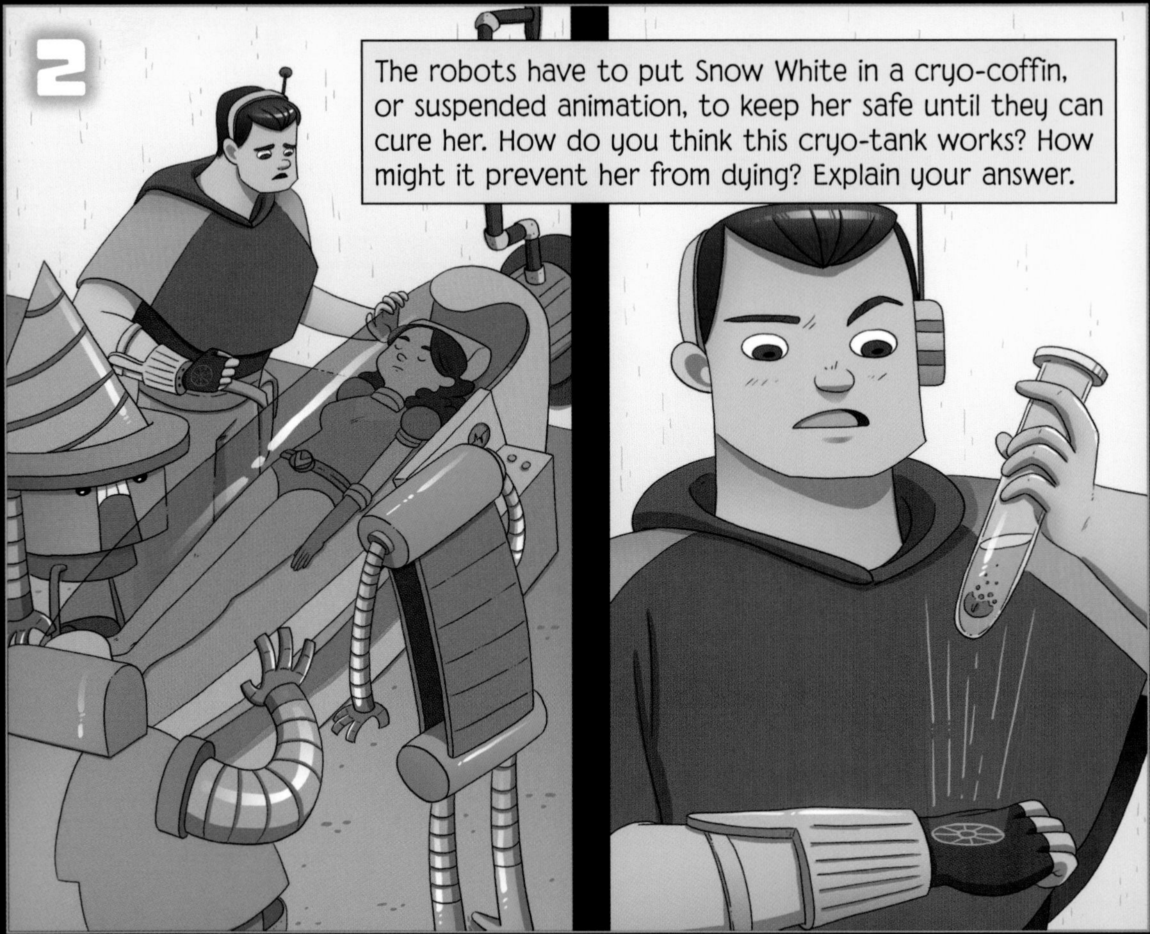
2
The robots have to put Snow White in a cryo-coffin, or suspended animation, to keep her safe until they can cure her. How do you think this cryo-tank works? How might it prevent her from dying? Explain your answer.

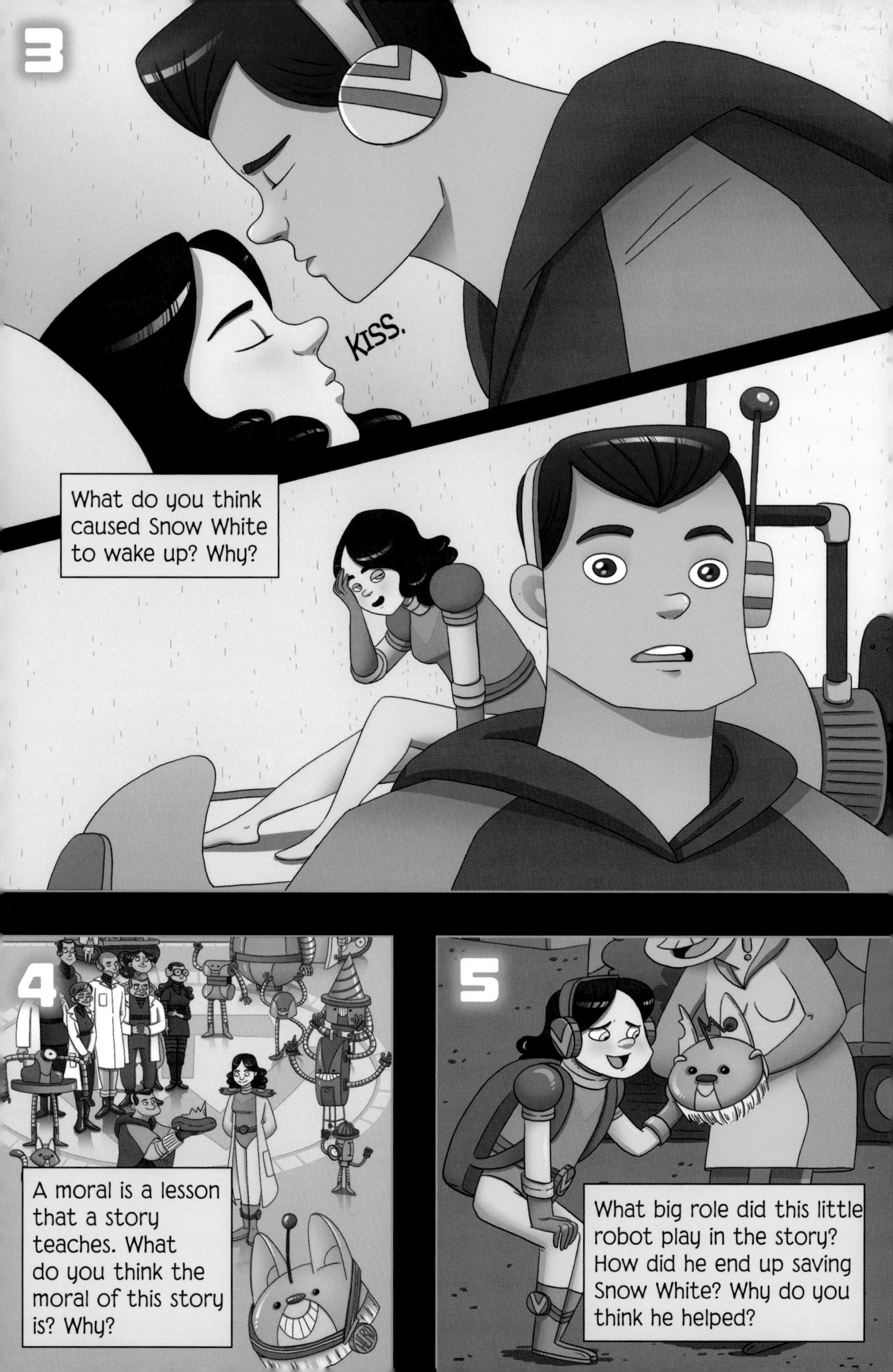
3
KISS.
What do you think caused Snow White to wake up? Why?
4
A moral is a lesson that a story teaches. What do you think the moral of this story is? Why?
5
What big role did this little robot play in the story? How did he end up saving Snow White? Why do you think he helped?

AUTHOR

Louise Simonson writes about monsters, science fiction and fantasy characters, and superheroes. She wrote the award-winning Power Pack series, several best-selling X-Men titles, Web of Spider-man for Marvel Comics, and Superman: Man of Steel and Steel for DC Comics. She has also written many books for kids. She is married to comic artist and writer Walter Simonson and lives in the suburbs of New York City.

ILLUSTRATOR

Jimena Sánchez was born in Mexico City, Mexico, in 1980. She studied illustration in the Escuela Nacional de Artes Plásticas (National School of Arts) and has since worked and lived in the United States as well as Spain. Jimena now lives in Mexico City again, working as an illustrator and comic book artist. Her art has appeared in many children's books and magazines.

GLOSSARY

align (uh-LAHYN)--to arrange things so that they form a line or are in proper position

apprentice (uh-PREN-tiss)--a person who learns a job or skill by working for a fixed period of time for someone who is good at that job or skill

aptitude (APP-ti-tood)--natural ability to do something or to learn something

brace (BRAYSS)--to get ready for something difficult or unpleasant

cure (KYOOR)--something (like a drug or medical treatment) that stops a disease and makes someone healthy again

formula (FOHR-myoo-luh)--a list of the ingredients used for making something (such as a medicine or a drink)

integrity (in-TEG-ruh-tee)--the quality of being honest and fair

malfunctioned (mal-FUHNK-shuhnd)--broke or failed to work properly

possess (puh-ZESS)--to have or own something

prospector (PRAH-spek-ter)--someone who searches the land for special or valuable minerals, rocks, gems, etc.

prosper (PROHSS-per)--to become very successful usually by making a lot of money

quarantine (KWAR-uhn-teen)--the situation of being kept away from others to prevent a disease from spreading

regent (REE-jent)--a person who rules a kingdom when the king or queen is not able to rule

stead (STED)--in place of something or someone

vain (VAYN)--too proud of yourself

AWESOMELY EVER AFTER.

FAR OUT FAIRY TALES
Ninja-rella
A GRAPHIC NOVEL
JOEY COMEAU
OMAR LOZANO

FAR OUT FAIRY TALES
RED RIDING HOOD, SUPERHERO
A GRAPHIC NOVEL
OTIS FRAMPTON

FAR OUT FAIRY TALES
SNOW WHITE AND THE SEVEN ROBOTS
A GRAPHIC NOVEL
LOUISE SIMONSON
JIMENA SANCHEZ

FAR OUT FAIRY TALES
SUPER BILLY GOATS GRUFF
A GRAPHIC NOVEL
SEAN TULIEN
FERNANDO CANO

FAR OUT FAIRY TALES

ONLY FROM STONE ARCH BOOKS!

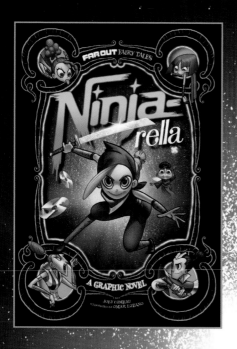

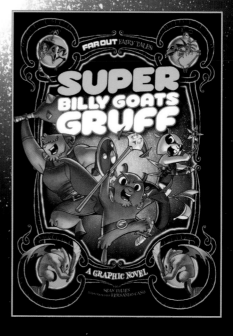